SHERLOCK HOLMES

AND THE GIANT RAT OF SUMATRA

By the same author

The Lost Files of Sherlock Holmes
The Chronicles of Sherlock Holmes

SHERLOCK HOLMES

AND THE GIANT RAT OF SUMATRA

Paul D. Gilbert

ROBERT HALE · LONDON

ISBN 978 0 7090 8904 9

Robert Hale Limited
Clerkenwell House
Clerkenwell Green
London EC1R 0HT

www.halebooks.com

4   6   8   10   9   7   5   3

Printed in Great Britain by MPG Books Group,
Bodmin and King's Lynn

CONTENTS

Part One – The Matilda Briggs

Part Two – The Giant Rat of Sumatra

INTRODUCTION

Of all of the unwritten tales that Sir Arthur Conan Doyle alluded to during the course of many of his wonderful stories, the one that seems to have fired the public's imagination more than any other are his references to the *Matilda Briggs* and the giant rat of Sumatra. This was a story for which he deemed the world to be as yet, unprepared!

I have already interpreted seven unwritten stories in my collection *The Chronicles of Sherlock Holmes* and I now humbly submit my own explanation of this dramatic-sounding reference, which Holmes mentioned to Watson during *The Adventure of The Sussex Vampire*.

I hope that my efforts are worthy of the kind of story that Sir Arthur might have written himself, had he decided to, and that you get as much pleasure from reading my interpretation as I have from writing it.

Once again I cannot emphasize enough the support and dedication that I have received from my wife Jackie, for which I will always be grateful.

Paul D. Gilbert

'Matilda Briggs was not the name of a young woman, Watson,' said Holmes in a reminiscent voice. 'It was the name of a ship which is associated with the giant rat of Sumatra, a story for which the world is not yet prepared.'

The Adventure of the Sussex Vampire
by Sir Arthur Conan Doyle

Part One

THE MATILDA BRIGGS

CHAPTER ONE

THE ART OF MEDITATION

During the course of those long weeks subsequent to Sherlock Holmes's traumatic encounter with Diego at St Jude's, which resulted in Holmes successfully saving the life of Isadora Persano,[1] I decided to remain in close attendance upon my friend.

As you may recall, Persano had been declared insane following his encounter with Diego's venomous worm and Holmes spent a long and harrowing night lying in wait for Persano's would be assailant. The awful sights and sounds that Holmes had been exposed to during his time spent within that dreadful asylum had had a profound effect upon his constitution, and I could only imagine the images that still plagued his mind. I shall forever be haunted by the look in his eyes as he sat by the window in Hanwell, staring vacantly up at the full grey moon.

Quite often, throughout these recent weeks, I had noticed that same look come upon him, and despite my best efforts at erasing his chronic despondency, I realized that his obsession with the subject would not be allayed. He would endlessly speculate as to how many of Persano's fellow inmates were, in actual fact, certifiably insane. Had the environment in which they had been incarcerated been one of the causes of their condition? Or, indeed, as in the case of Persano, had other inhuman forms of treatment been administered to the patients, serving only to compound their sorry state? In any event the sounds of their wailing, which had echoed throughout those stark unforgiving halls, conveyed to Holmes their great suffering rather than any mental illness.

I became convinced that Holmes's inability to release himself from the horrors of St Jude's was born of a very real fear for his own sanity. His mental faculties were as finely tuned as the rarest Stradivarius and he was more aware than I of the dangers of over-tuning any instrument, the result – a broken string!

During my long association with Sherlock Holmes I had been witness on many occasions to the great lengths he was willing to go to in his endless search for justice. A dozen times or more I had to reproach him for over-extending himself, both physically and mentally in his unremitting pursuit. Several times I had sadly been proved correct in my diagnosis and this had led to extended sabbaticals and convalescence. Even though he was supposed to rest when these holidays took place, many a time he stumbled across other problems, which required his amazing skills. One such case was that of the 'Devil's Foot'[2] which was the name of a deadly African root, and its effects almost succeeded in sending Holmes to an asylum permanently.

Thankfully, on each occasion a new mystery or fresh adventure would soon present itself and a miraculous transformation would take place that seemed to revitalize his every sinew. For so long as his mind was employed in solving a new problem, his body and soul would be energized. All thoughts of rest and inactivity would be immediately dispelled.

The situation in which he now found himself, however, was different from any other to which I had, so far, been witness. It was almost as if the 'string' had finally snapped. Each time that I tried to divert him, either with news of a possible crime or even just an item of curiosity from *The Times*, he would show an interest for a moment or two before relapsing into his intense reverie. That forlorn look would return to his eyes once more, and I felt as if I had lost him again. But I would not be defeated. My mission both as a man of medicine and, more important, as a friend was to convince him that his fear was unfounded and that the law-abiding public at large was in need of a Sherlock Holmes at the peak of his powers. I was shocked to realize on this occasion that even his self-belief would not motivate him.

Then my mind turned to still darker thoughts. Had his long-dormant habit of injecting himself with a seven per cent solution of cocaine surfaced once again? Was his downward spiral to continue, out of control? With a sense of both guilt and betrayal, tempered by a touch of self-righteousness, I allowed myself a surreptitious glance into the top drawer of his desk. To my intense relief I found that the lid of his thin leather syringe box lay undisturbed. I was certain of this for the fine veil of dust that had been evident on the last such occasion was still present. I had barely the time to close the drawer once more, before Holmes returned from his toilet. I noticed his arched right eyebrow with a feeling of dread.

'So!' Holmes began in a stronger and more familiar voice than he had been employing of late. 'It would seem that the ever-watchful doctor has added distrust to his crime of constant meddling!' His tone became bitter.

'Whatever do you mean?' I turned away from his glare in an effort to conceal my guilt, but this was surely in vain.

'Oh Watson.' Holmes slowly shook his head and his tone was more one of sympathy than reprimand. 'Just as you always ascertain that there is a thin layer of dust across the lid of my leather box, so do I ensure that the key to that drawer is always left at an unusual angle, impossible to replicate at random. As my box is the only object within this drawer, I would have to be the world's poorest amateur consulting detective were I not to be aware of your prying!'

'Even in your present state of malaise it seems impossible for me to deceive you.' I turned back towards him, my face visibly reddening as I did so. Then, to my great surprise and I might add, my intense relief, for the first time in many weeks I heard the sound of my old friend's laughter.

'My dear fellow, do not be so embarrassed for I know full well that your actions were well intentioned. Besides which your suspicions were unfounded. I am slowly dispelling the fears that grew within me from my night in St Judes, by a more natural and effective means.' At this moment Holmes filled his long cherry-wood pipe from the Persian slipper on our mantelpiece and I knew, from this, that he was in a more contemplative mood than he had been of late.

'By what means would that be?' I asked whilst pulling a chair up to the fire and filling a pipe of my own.

It was several minutes before Holmes eventually replied, for he was visibly enjoying every long, relaxed draw that he took from his pipe.

'Why, by the most ancient and effective means possible.' Holmes smiled at my puzzled look. 'I speak of meditation, of course!'

It might be as well to mention here that meditation was just one of the many processes and methods that Holmes had employed throughout his career as the world's foremost and most renowned consulting, amateur detective. As his associate and chronicler I had been privileged to witness many of the problems presented to him and their resolution. Observation and deduction were the key words that he used to describe his method, yet quite often he used his instinct and imagination. He often berated the regular forces for being somewhat sadly lacking in these attributes, Inspector Lestrade of Scotland Yard in particular. However, on more than one occasion I had been witness to Holmes's ability to trace the thought processes of his quarry by following the chain of events in his own mind, based upon the subject's mental abilities and state of mind at the time of the crime's execution.

Alternatively, when such data were not available to him he would sit motionless for hours on end and, to the eyes of an uninitiated witness, go into a state of deep trance. However, this was not simply a matter of emptying his mind of all thoughts: only of those that he deemed to be irrelevant. A prime example of this would be the culmination of the strange affair of *The Man with the Twisted Lip*. On this occasion, whilst staying over night at the villa of Neville St Clair at Lee, in Kent, Holmes had perched himself upon an Eastern-style divan that he had constructed from as many cushions and pillows as he was able to collect. As he had sat there with his legs crossed, he selected a point upon the ceiling at which to concentrate his gaze. For as many hours as I had slept in the bed opposite, so Holmes smoked an entire ounce of shag tobacco through his old brier pipe, and sat motionless and awake throughout the entire night! By the time that the day's first light had appeared, Holmes was in possession of the solution.

'Besides, what is insanity?' Holmes broke in upon my thoughts with this most startling of questions. 'Is a blind man insane because he cannot see? Is a crippled man insane because he cannot walk? Of course not! An insane man is not one who cannot think, he suffers from the inability to think clearly. By meditating it is possible to recognize all of our thoughts but only to focus on those that are relevant and allow the others gently to float harmlessly away. However, it is also desirable to remain in a state of full awareness whilst doing so. A prime example, of course, was that night we spent at Lee, in Kent.' Holmes stopped abruptly so that he could observe the look of amazement on my face.

He was not to be disappointed. It was almost as if he had broken in upon my innermost thoughts and I told him so. 'Is this devilry also the result of your meditation?' I asked breathlessly.

A brief smile played about his thin lips before he replied.

'No, not at all, old fellow. I just know my Watson. When I first mentioned the word meditation I observed you glance away as you fell into a chain of deep thought. You tried to remember an occasion when I had employed meditation as a means for solving a past case. Your furrowed brow indicated that you were having difficulty in doing this. Your eyes then turned to the shelf on which you keep your copies of those lamentably dramatic chronicles of our previous adventures. Of course! *The Man with the Twisted Lip*. Your look of confusion transformed into one of triumph and, as a way of confirming this, your eyes moved around the room, from cushion to cushion as you recalled how I had constructed my divan at Lee, in Kent. In conclusion, you suddenly became irritated as you glanced at the clock and remembered at what unearthly time I had awakened you.'

'Holmes, it was four-thirty in the morning!' I protested.

Holmes slapped his thigh in triumphant glee when my outburst had confirmed the truth of his reconstruction.

'Now admit it, I was correct on every point.' Holmes laughed.

'Well, the effects of your night at St Jude's have certainly done nothing to dampen your faculties,' I grudgingly confirmed. 'I would also say that there is much to commend the art of meditation, for surely you are transformed!'

'High praise, indeed, for the oldest spiritual method in the world,' Holmes sarcastically retorted. 'I may have informed you of the extended time that I spent in Tibet, during the course of the three-year sabbatical that I imposed, immediately after my confrontation with Colonel Moriarty at the Reichenbach Falls.'

'I recall that you spent some months in the company of the Dalai Lama,' I confirmed.

Holmes nodded solemnly as he lit his cherry-wood again.

'It was during my stay there that I became fully aware of the limitless capabilities and potentials of the human mind. I experienced the innermost peace that can be obtained by merely concentrating and meditating upon the breath. I observed the heights of spiritual enlightenment that the Dalai Lama and his monks were capable of reaching as the result of years of such practice. I was not able to reach even a fraction of those heights and yet I became convinced of their belief that the average man uses barely one tenth of his mental potential; some, of course, not even that!' Holmes added mischievously.

'How did you become so convinced of the validity of this startling assertion?' I then asked.

Holmes glanced briefly towards me, no doubt to ascertain whether mine had been a genuine enquiry, or merely an expression of my cynicism.

'Watson,' Holmes began in reply, evidently convinced of my sincerity, 'I actually witnessed these monks perform the arts of levitation and astral travel!'

'Levitation is a phenomenon that I have heard of, although I would have to witness this myself to become wholly convinced of its validity, but what in heaven's name is astral travel?'

'By unlocking a further proportion of his mental capabilities, it is possible for the practitioner to transport himself to any location of his choosing, regardless of distance, without his body moving a single inch! Before you question me further,' Holmes rapidly continued, to forestall my interrupting him, 'I will tell you that the monks' descriptions of the places they had visited during the course of this travelling were extraordinary in their accuracy, and beyond the reach of their physical circumstances. It is an area upon which I have barely scratched the surface, but yet my limited experiences will allow me to embark on my latest monograph and you to proceed with your long-planned fishing trip, safe in the knowledge that I am to be gainfully employed throughout your absence.'

'How will you entitle your latest work?' I asked.

'It shall be known as: *The Art of Meditation and its Employment in the Detection of Crime,*' Holmes proudly announced.

Then the meaning of his previous statement suddenly dawned on me. 'I was not aware that I had indicated in any way my intention to go fishing!' I ventured.

'You have not directly, but I observed you receive a letter some weeks back from your old school friend, Cresswell, who owns a small plot in Shropshire that contains a short section of a famous trout stream. I have seen you successively crumple then carefully fold this letter many times whilst you have battled with your conscience over the nature of your long-overdue reply. Despite the wet and inclement weather that we have been subjected to of late, when I see you re-oil your waders I naturally deduce that you intend to reply to Cresswell in the affirmative.'

I slowly shook my head in disbelief. 'My goodness, Holmes, I am continually amazed by the things that you remember and observe. I cannot believe that I thought you to be unwell.'

'Do not admonish yourself, Watson, for your diagnosis has been a correct one. However I merely wish to assure you that you can let me out of your sight now without my getting up to any mischief. My monograph will surely occupy any of my surplus mental energy and I am certain that Mrs Hudson will keep me adequately sustained.' Holmes smiled at my continued reticence. 'You must send your reply without delay!'

'Well ... if you are certain?'

I lost no time in following my friend's instructions and it was arranged that I should depart for Shropshire on the following Tuesday. Any misgivings that I might still have regarding abandoning Holmes were soon dispelled by the sight of him feverishly burrowing his way through swaths of files and notepaper, with which he liberally festooned our room.

Indeed, so engrossed had Holmes become in his latest endeavour that I began to wonder whether he would even notice my eventual departure! Any attempts that I made at conversation were met by either grunts or snarls, accompanied by the perpetual sound of Holmes's pencil scratching in his notebook.

When the morning of my departure eventually arrived Holmes dismissed me with a cursory wave over his shoulder whilst he laboured at his desk. Consequently I hurried to my waiting cab without a tinge of regret.

I was well met at Diddlebury station by a fine trap and pair that Cresswell had kindly arranged for me, and soon we were traversing some charming countryside on our way to Delbury Hall.

The hall itself, dating from the early years of the century, was a fine square building of red brick, with a small wing on either side. It was reached by way of a short, bush-lined gravel drive that circled the beautiful lake, which was fed by the object of my sporting quest, namely the River Diddle, although in reality it was little more than a fast-running stream.

Cresswell's wife Elizabeth evidently did not share her husband's enthusiasm for my visit. Whereas he was warm and gracious as he greeted me on my arrival in the trap, she was cold and indifferent, dispatching a young groom to take my bags to my room with a most disdainful wave. I was disappointed to discover, upon reaching the room, that I had been relegated to the left wing, which afforded a view no more rewarding than the small stable house at the rear of the main building. After I had unpacked I sank on to my hard, uncomfortable bed and consoled myself with the thought of my beautiful surroundings and the days of good sport that lay ahead.

Our small but adequate evening meal was taken in cold silence and my mood only improved once Elizabeth had taken herself to her room under the pretext of a headache. Thereupon Cresswell and I indulged ourselves in some entertaining reminiscences and a port that was well above average. Sadly Cresswell could not join me at the river in the morning as he had to give his urgent attention to some cases; as a fellow doctor, it was a situation with which I could easily sympathise. However, the Diddle more than lived up to its reputation and by lunchtime I had a fine brace of brown trout to take back to the hall. The elderly cook, Mrs Bumstead, kindly prepared them for our evening meal and it was only upon their consumption that Elizabeth warmed at last to my visit.

The remainder of my stay, as a consequence, was a positive delight. The glass remained high, the weather fine and the trout continued to respond well to my trusty flies. By the end of the week Elizabeth and I had become firm friends and she stood and waved to me as the trap departed for the station. The greeting that I received from Holmes did nothing to dampen my mood. Evidently the completion of his monograph had filled him with a renewed energy and enthusiasm and he could not wait to read it to me, which was necessary as the writing of the first draft was illegible to anyone but himself.

Although his work contained many points of interest it was true to say that his dry, academic style would only hold the interest of the most ardent students of the subject. Sadly, the country air and the long journey home had left me most grateful for the comfort of my chair and after but a few pages of Holmes's drone I found myself drifting off into a deep slumber.

Fortunately Holmes was not unsympathetic to my obvious fatigue and he dispatched me to my room with the not entirely comforting assurance that he would continue with his reading as soon as breakfast had been cleared away the following morning.

Therefore my relief at discovering that a most fateful letter had arrived with our first post might well be understood.

CHAPTER TWO

THE MATILDA BRIGGS

Surprisingly Holmes appeared to be somewhat crestfallen at the letter's arrival, as breakfast had been completed and he was about to resume his reading when Mrs Hudson arrived to clear the table and deliver our post.

Holmes tore impatiently into the envelopes. Two bills and a letter of gratitude from a former client soon found their way on to the floor. The contents of the fourth envelope, however, were treated somewhat differently and Holmes soon passed the letter across to me for my opinion. The draft for his monograph lay forgotten on the arm of his chair.

The letter was short on content and detail and as businesslike as one would expect from a firm of City solicitors. Morrison, Morrison & Dodd specialized in maritime affairs and, as some readers might recall, would subsequently lead us upon the adventure of *The Sussex Vampire*. However, on this occasion the subject matter of their letter appeared, at first glance, to be altogether more mundane. I read the letter aloud to Holmes:

Dear Mr Holmes,
Inspector Lestrade of Scotland Yard has passed your name to us with his recommendation that you are the most successful and discreet of any consulting detective that he has encountered. The

extraordinary nature of our problem, will, he is certain, entice you into acting on our behalf. Lestrade has offered to call upon you to explain the finer details, as our clients, the owners of the steam clipper, the *Matilda Briggs*, wish to avoid public knowledge of this scandal. Please visit the vessel at Canary Wharf, where it lies abandoned, as a matter of the greatest urgency.

Yours sincerely,

James Morrison.

This cursory communication had been signed by the company's senior partner.

'Finer details, indeed! 'Holmes exploded. 'There are no details here at all!'

'Apart from the simple fact that the *Matilda Briggs* has been deserted and now lies abandoned. Surely that extraordinary fact alone is most worthy of note,' I suggested, whereupon I immediately dived into our directories. From our copy of Lloyd's Register, I was able to ascertain that the *Matilda Briggs* was one of the first steam tea clippers to enter service and that, to this day, she holds the record for the fastest journey a clipper has made from Calcutta to London. From a legal register I found out that our prospective clients were a firm of well-established solicitors with a reputation for great discretion.

'Crumbs, Watson! I am being fed nothing but crumbs. To think that I have to rely on that fool Lestrade for any information that might aid me in this case.' As he spoke, Holmes strode over to the mantelpiece and began filling his first pipe of the day.

'So you already regard this letter as the beginning of a case,' I asked speculatively.

'As you know, Watson, I am loath to make any assumptions before being in possession of the facts. Although in this instance there are no facts at all, other than an abandoned vessel. Any hope that I hold of a worthwhile examination by an investigator possessed of my abilities lies in the fact that it is impossible for a vessel to arrive at a London dock with nobody on board. We must await the arrival of that scourge of London criminals.' Holmes finished this statement with more than a hint of sarcasm and began pacing the room while an endless plume of smoke pumped from his old clay pipe.

When Lestrade did eventually arrive, he was in a state of great agitation. Holmes greeted him with a feigned indifference that belied his earlier impatience. We sent down for coffee and once Mrs Hudson had been bundled from the room Holmes threw the letter from Morrison across the room to Lestrade.

'Since when did my humble practice rely on recommendations from Scotland Yard?' Holmes asked sharply.

'I am certain that it does not, Mr Holmes, but if this little mystery is not right up your alley then I am sure that I do not know what is!' Lestrade replied with surprising spirit.

'As you might know, I depend on hearing the facts at first hand from my clients in order that I should obtain a full understanding of the matter.' Holmes stood over Lestrade and waved his finger accusingly. 'This letter tells me nothing!' he boomed. He clasped his sinewy fingers together behind his back and turned away from Lestrade, towards the window. Lestrade's withering glare at me showed he was aghast at Holmes's ill temper, but I could only offer a shrug by way of consolation.

As if sensing this brief, furtive exchange behind his back, Holmes's tone mellowed considerably when he next spoke.

'Despite this less than auspicious beginning, perhaps if you lay the facts before me in a clear and orderly manner this may yet be a matter of some minor interest to me.'

'That would be most good of you, Mr Holmes,' Lestrade responded, visibly relieved.

'Although at this stage I will commit myself to nothing!' Holmes warned as he sat down, cross-legged, upon his chair.

With a dramatic wave of his arm he invited Lestrade to speak and then, to aid his concentration, he closed his eyes and pressed his right forefinger to his lips.

Simultaneously Lestrade and I took out our notebooks, his to read from, and my own to make notes upon for Holmes's subsequent perusal.

'Gentlemen, the basic facts are these,' Lestrade began. 'Yesterday morning, at approximately half past four, two dock workers arrived for work at Canary Wharf, to discover that a supposedly empty berth was now being occupied by the tea cutter, the *Matilda Briggs*. Surprising as her presence undoubtedly was, still more confusing was the fact that she was not tethered. It was concluded that she had, therefore, drifted randomly into that position. It was subsequently discovered that she had been due to dock two days earlier but at a berth much further downstream. Her late arrival was causing some concern because she is considered to be one of the fastest and most reliable craft in the entire merchant fleet! At the time the reason for her delay was unknown, so that when the dock workers saw her name on the hull they immediately summoned the harbour master.

'The vessel was boarded at once and to everyone's astonishment the only crew member on board was a young cabin boy, Carlo Maddalena, who appeared to be on the point of death. He died shortly afterwards in hospital and a nurse heard the boy say with his dying breath: 'Death himself has surely come for us all!'

'Not another soul, alive or dead, could be found on board and not a clue as to their fate. Morrison, Morrison and Dodd are acting on behalf of the ship's insurers and although the Yard will be conducting its own investigations, the insurers have requested an independent inquiry by yourself. Those are the only known facts at this time, gentlemen.' It was with some relief that Lestrade put away his notebook and he lit a cigarette as soon as he had done so.

Holmes slowly unravelled himself and lit a cigarette of his own.

'I really must congratulate you on the concise precision of your notes, Lestrade,' Holmes surprisingly announced. 'I presume that you have already visited the ship?'

'You presume correctly, Mr Holmes, although I might have saved myself the bother for all the good that it did me,' Lestrade responded bitterly.

'Inspector, all the effort in the world, if channelled in the wrong direction, will always be of little benefit, in the same way as the untrained eye can see everything and yet understand nothing at all. Yet we should always be bothered, otherwise our very existence is meaningless. Were there no traces of the ship's log? Although, of course, had there been you would not feel the need to consult with me now.'

Lestrade shook his head disconsolately. 'As you say, Mr Holmes, there would have been no real mystery.'

'Were there no clues to be found in the ship's inventory?' I asked.

'Sadly that appears to have vanished, together with the log.'

'Well, whoever is responsible for the *Matilda Briggs* mystery certainly did their job most thoroughly,' I commented quietly.

'Yet are you so certain that the ill-fated young man was indeed the cabin boy?' Holmes asked of Lestrade.

'Fortunately the crew register was the only documentation that was beyond the reach of the culprit. It was lodged with the harbour master before the ship's departure.'

'Are there no clues as to the fate of the remainder of the crew? If pirates had attacked the ship for example, there would have been obvious signs of violence to be found on board,' I suggested. I observed Holmes smile proudly in my direction as I posed this question to Lestrade.

'That notion had occurred to us, but there were no indications of bloodshed or disturbance of any sort. Although ...' Lestrade's voice trailed away thoughtfully.

All this while Holmes had been prowling around the room restlessly while drawing on his cigarette. However, upon Lestrade's hesitation he turned round, levelling the cigarette in his direction. 'Tell me, Inspector; no matter how irrelevant or trivial this might appear to be to you now, might its significance become apparent once we have accumulated more data?'

'Well, there were some unusual marks or symbols etched deeply into the decking just a few feet away from where the cabin boy had fallen. We could find no implement nearby that could have made these marks, so we have concluded that the cabin boy could not have been their creator. Their meaning, however, remains unknown.'

'Think, man! Did these markings remind you of anything?' Holmes insisted.

Lestrade shook his head disconsolately. 'No, nothing at all. They might have been a crude kind of lettering, I suppose, but from an alphabet that I am not familiar with. However, I have arranged to meet Mr Dodd at the *Matilda Briggs* this afternoon, so you may reach your own conclusions then.'

'Did the markings appear to have been made recently?' Holmes asked thoughtfully. He turned towards the window, apparently searching for inspiration from the grey skies above the streets.

'Yes, now you mention it, they did. The wood that had been exposed was considerably lighter in tone than the remainder,' Lestrade replied, as if surprised at this conclusion that Holmes's questioning had drawn from him.

'I shall make a detective of you yet, Inspector!'

'Holmes, you seem to be implying that someone took the time to inscribe nonsensical etchings into the deck of the ship whilst some unspeakable drama was being enacted all around them. I do not understand why you are attaching such importance to them,' I said.

'It is precisely because they are there when common sense tells us that they should not be, that I attach significance to them. Besides, we should not assume that they are nonsensical simply because the good inspector and his men cannot understand their meaning. As you know, I will reach no conclusions until I have put everything to the test.'

'Does the body of the cabin boy display any obvious signs of violence?' I enquired.

'There were some unusual blemishes about the boy's neck but nothing that suggests foul play.' Again Lestrade shook his head.

'Although his untimely demise would certainly suggest as much. Is Carlo Maddalena still to be found in the hospital?' Holmes asked.

'The post mortem is being carried out at Middlesex Street.'

'Excellent! Then that shall be our first port of call. Mrs Hudson!' Holmes called out, at once. Upon her replying he requested that she procure us a cab.

'Now steady on, Mr Holmes.' Lestrade stood up to protest at Holmes's impulsive plans. 'Are we going to abandon Mr Dodd at the quayside?'

On his way to get his coat Holmes suddenly stopped in his tracks and addressed Lestrade face to face. 'Inspector Lestrade, Mr Dodd and the *Matilda Briggs* will still be available to us tomorrow, whereas, as the good doctor here will confirm, the body of the cabin boy will not become any fresher over night! I suggest that we make our way to Middlesex Street without another moment's delay. Oh, and Doctor, be good enough to bring your bag.' Holmes issued this instruction as he bounded from the room towards the street below.

As I made my way to my room, to retrieve the said bag, I paused to reflect on the stark change that had come over Holmes since the arrival of the letter from Morrison, Morrison & Dodd. All thoughts of his informative but dry monograph had been put to one side and the demons of his night at St Jude's had truly been exorcised. Such were the effects of stimulating work on his finely balanced mind.

I hastened my step as he called out once more.

Our cab made ponderous progress through some unusually heavy traffic, which allowed me time to reflect upon the fate of the *Matilda Briggs*'s crew. Had there been a disease or plague on board? Perhaps the bodies had then been thrown overboard to avoid the spread of further infection until only the cabin boy remained alive. At the last even he had succumbed and the only clue remaining was the marks on the boy's neck.

On the other hand, Holmes's earlier questioning of Lestrade seemed to suggest that foul play was a possibility that he was considering. To my way of thinking this seemed the less likely notion; after all, had not Lestrade already stated that there were no other signs of violence visible on board? Besides, who or what could be capable of wiping out and disposing of an entire ship's crew?

Perhaps a mutiny might have resulted in the crew's annihilation. If that had been the case, however, how would the sole survivor have been capable of disposing of the bodies in the weakened state in which he had been found? Indeed, would he even have had the presence of mind to consider destroying the captain's log? What would have been his motive for so doing? Unless, of course, he had been the instigator of the mutiny himself. Then that explanation did seem to be most unlikely also.

And so, as we approached the hospital, I had come full circle and back to my original notion of a virulent infectious disease. I decided to voice this in order that we three should approach the cabin boy's body with extreme caution.

'Watson,' Holmes responded, 'there is much merit to your notion that a disease wiped out the entire crew of the Matilda Briggs. However, it does contain one profound flaw....'

'So, pray tell, what would that be exactly?' I could not contain myself on this occasion, because I was so certain that my reasoning was sound and for so long I had endured Holmes's self-opinionated dismissal of any theories of mine that varied from his own ideas.

'After all,' I continued, though in a calmer tone than I had previously employed, 'Lestrade's evidence indicates that no violent action took place aboard ship.'

'Perhaps there are no obvious indications of violence, Watson,' Holmes replied quietly. 'However, there are more subtle ways of bringing about an untimely death than spraying some blood around by using a machete! Besides, you are giving the cabin boy's dying words absolutely no credence at all.'

'*Death himself has surely come for us all,*' I mumbled reflectively, while I admitted to myself that while I had engrossed myself in all my theorizing, the words of the cabin boy had, indeed, slipped my mind.

'Remember, Watson, that when I disposed of Colonel Moriarty at the Reichenbach Falls, I did so without leaving a single mark upon his body. Nor was there any spillage of blood.'

'Ah, but you employed the Japanese martial art of baritsu.'

'Exactly!'

'I think that I now understand why you are always so reluctant to voice your hypotheses before you are in full possession of the facts,' I admitted, to Holmes's obvious satisfaction.

'Theories and notions, indeed! A simple examination of the cabin boy's body will surely enlighten one of you soon enough,' Lestrade said in a strangely exasperated tone. It suddenly occurred to me that we had not heard a single word from our companion throughout the entire journey to Middlesex Street. Yet, when he did eventually speak, it was of great surprise to both Holmes and myself that his words proved to be so profound. Neither of us could think of a single response and the remainder of our journey was continued in silence.

CHAPTER THREE

THE SHIP OF GHOSTS

Lestrade's presence ensured that there was no delay in our being shown through to the hospital's large and crowded mortuary. It was in a solemn silence that we approached the slab on which Carlo Maddalena had been laid, for it was only now, as we gazed down upon his youthful countenance, that we realized just how young the final victim of the tragedy appeared to be.

Even the stone-grey pallor of death had done little to diminish the innocence of his round and cheery features. My short-lived experience of service as an army surgeon during the Afghan campaign, and my subsequent association with Holmes, had presented me with aspects of death in its many and varied forms. Even so, I am strangely proud of the fact that my sensitivity to such sights had not been hardened by these experiences. I noted that even Holmes was clearly moved by the sight and gestured for me to approach the young man with my bag while he and Lestrade stood back.

I moved gingerly but most thoroughly upwards from the feet, but discovered nothing of note until I reached the young man's neck. I was duty-bound to concur with the findings of the police surgeon, in that the only visible possible cause of death was two large bruises at the front of the neck. Obviously, as rigor mortis had set in, the original colour of the bruises was impossible to determine. The only thing that I could say with any certainty was that there was no damage to the skin and that the injury was internal. The blemishes were certainly not caused by any poison or illness that I could recognize. Not surprisingly, my findings were shifting my opinions more and more towards those of my friend.

I was on the point of standing upright, once more, when my eyes fell upon two small curved marks that were almost indiscernible, positioned an inch or two above each of the larger marks. I beckoned Holmes to join me and noticed, with some amusement, how a tentative Lestrade reluctantly followed suit, peering around Holmes's shoulder at the object of our attention. Holmes barely gave these new discoveries a moment's consideration before turning on his heel and striding from the room.

In a state of some confusion I bundled up the contents of my bag and soon followed after Holmes, eventually finding him waiting impatiently for me in the cab outside the hospital. We could not move off immediately as Lestrade still had some official business to conclude inside, so I took Holmes to task for his unusual behaviour in the mortuary.

'Well, I must say, Holmes, you could not have been more indifferent to my discoveries even if you had tried! Are they really of so little relevance?' I asked.

'On the contrary, Doctor, they are of the greatest significance; however there really was no necessity for me to examine them with closer attention, for I had already expected them to be there!' He uttered these astonishing words with an airiness that was irksome in the extreme.

'Surely you realize that the shape of these marks indicates that the poor young fellow was killed by nothing more than the inside of a man's hand. The smaller marks, which I so very nearly missed, were certainly made by the culprit's fingertips. I would have thought that this fact alone was worthy of note?' I implored.

Holmes turned sympathetically towards me once he had realized how his apparent dismissiveness seemed to belittle my findings.

'My dear fellow, your examination has now placed this case on an entirely different footing, for the perpetrator of those blows is undoubtedly a most singularly skilled and dangerous individual. Each one of those marks fell upon a fatal pressure point and for a blow of that force to land on each one of those with such deadly effect, indicates to me that we are dealing with a skilled master of the deadly arts. As to how such a person happened to be upon a deserted ship and why he should attack a helpless cabin boy are matters that I refuse to be drawn upon at such an early stage.'

These last words of Holmes were obviously designed to forestall my next barrage of questions. However, this was now academic for at that moment Lestrade rejoined us and a subtle gesture from Holmes suggested to me that he was not as yet prepared to share this new information with the good inspector.

'Well, Mr Holmes,' Lestrade chuckled quietly, 'you seem to have learnt as little from the examination of the corpse as the rest of us.'

'That, Inspector, remains to be seen!' Holmes sternly rebuked Lestrade and with that he rapped on the roof of the cab with his cane to stir the driver into motion. Lestrade promised to arrange for us to meet Mr Dodd at Canary Wharf on the following afternoon and we diverted to allow him out at Scotland Yard on our way to Baker Street. I remained there only long enough to down a welcome cognac, for mine had not been the most pleasant of experiences, before continuing to my surgery where I had some work that could not be neglected for a moment longer.

I was occupied for the remainder of the day and as a consequence did not see my friend again until the time of our appointment on the following afternoon. I arrived at the wharf promptly at two o'clock, only to be confronted by two of Lestrade's largest and most saturnine constables who would not let me pass until they had received a cursory nod from their superior.

Lestrade waved for me to join him at the quayside where he was standing next to a most singular-looking individual, whom I correctly assumed to be our prospective client.

Alistair Dodd, of Morrison, Morrison & Dodd was a man in his mid fifties, of average height, whose long black frock-coat did nothing to disguise how rotund he really was. This was also evident in his corpulent face which was decorated with an absurdly dark, coiled moustache that was positively dripping with pomade! This he was constantly twisting impatiently with the fingers of his right hand, which caused me to consider twice before I extended my own to him. His handshake was as weak and oily as I had anticipated and I wasted no time in releasing my grip. He hardly gave me a glance as he pointed towards the ship in front of us.

'Apparently we have been prohibited from going on board!' Dodd protested. 'I must say, Doctor Watson, that your associate holds a mighty high opinion of himself. He does not wish to run the risk of our disturbing any clues that he might discover. Clues indeed, stuff and nonsense if you ask me! After all, Inspector Lestrade here is a professional policeman!'

'He is also very aware of Mr Holmes's methods and, I am certain, that he would be more than willing to attest to the miraculous success that his methods have always yielded!' I rejoined, determined to defend my friend to the hilt. .

'I have no difficulty in confirming everything that the doctor has told you, Mr Dodd, and I am certain that none of us would be standing here this afternoon were it not the case.' I felt strangely proud of Lestrade at his defence of Holmes in his absence and I was on the point of telling him so when Holmes suddenly summoned me to board the *Matilda Briggs*. I did so somewhat sheepishly, for Holmes had also insisted that I come alone.

'His effrontery is intolerable!' Dodd blustered. 'You would do well to warn Mr Holmes that my patience is wearing somewhat thin and that should this tomfoolery of his continue for much longer, I shall seriously consider advising my clients to seek assistance from another source.' I acknowledged this advice by sarcastically doffing my hat in Dodd's direction, then I slowly began ascending the gangplank, leaving him still twisting his ridiculous moustache.

As I came upon the deck, I could understand at once the cause of Dodd's confusion at the investigative techniques of my friend. He was stretched out, lying flat on his stomach, with his right hand raised above his head as if he was shielding his eyes from a non-existent glare.

'Really Holmes,' I began, 'you really cannot afford to be so cavalier towards our client if—' Holmes was determined not to hear another word upon the subject.

'Watson!' he warned me. 'Now, would you be good enough to pass me down a sheet or two of your notepaper and a sharp, stout pencil?' Then, in answer to my questioning glance, he added: 'I wish to take some rubbings from this piece of decking.'

I was on the point of querying this request when I remembered Lestrade's reference to a set of strange but irrelevant markings that he had noticed during his own examination of the ship. Evidently Holmes was attaching more importance to these carvings than his professional counterpart.

As I stood there, staring down at Holmes, I suddenly became aware that the stiff autumnal breeze was being chilled by its sweeping across the broad expanse of the Thames. I immediately turned up the collar of my coat to guard against it and lit up a cigarette with some difficulty.

By the time that Holmes had completed his rubbings our client's patience had become exhausted. He and Lestrade arrived on deck just as Holmes was brushing himself down.

Dodd's plump features were reddened by his impatience and Holmes could barely suppress a mischievous smile as he cheerily greeted the two of them on board. 'You really should not upset yourself, Mr Dodd, Watson and Lestrade will tell you that my methods are not always of the most conventional. However, any hope that I may have had of unravelling your little mystery would have been made that much harder had the two of you added your own footmarks to those that have already confused the issue.'

'Well, I must say! Little mystery indeed!' Dodd exploded.

'Perhaps I am not doing full justice to the problem with this flippant description of mine. For this could well prove to be one of the most challenging cases that I have ever been involved in and it is certainly unique in the annals of crime. Now please, gentlemen, kindly allow me to continue with my work.' With that, Holmes turned his back on the two of them and threw himself down on to the deck once again.

This time he took out his lens and began slithering around on the boards like a viper in pursuit of its prey. Every so often he would pause for a moment or two and examine something or other with minute diligence. Occasionally he would emit a loud grunt of disappointment. Then again he might laugh to himself as he made a more positive discovery although, of course, the nature of each find would remain a mystery to the rest of us for some time to come.

After a while he paused from his reptilian motions and withdrew a small buff envelope from his inside pocket. He gestured for me to hold this open while he then proceeded to shuffle together a small pile of what appeared to be dark and dusty grain from the deck. He then poured this delicately into the envelope with as much care as if he had been handling gold dust.

Once he had brushed himself down for a second time Holmes proceeded to examine every inch of the polished handrails with his glass while I began to sense Dodd's growing impatience. At last, when Holmes paused to light a cigarette, Dodd could contain himself no longer. He addressed himself quietly to Lestrade but at a level just loud enough for Holmes to overhear.

'I must confess, Inspector, that based on this first evidence, I am not altogether convinced that employing Mr Holmes and his so-called method is in the best interests of my clients. Surely his glowing reputation is pure hyperbole and if the best we can come up with in the next few days is an envelope full of dust, then I will advise my clients accordingly.'

'That, sir, is your privilege,' Lestrade responded. 'However, this is a criminal matter and I am duty bound to take the best advice that is available to me. For all that his ways are unconventional, which I do not always approve of, Mr Holmes has rarely failed in his unorthodox investigations.

'Thank you, Lestrade.' Holmes smiled broadly through a thick plume of smoke. 'I can assure you both, however, that I shall get to the bottom of this matter with or without Mr Dodd's approval! Now I shall conclude my examination of the ship below decks. Alone! 'Holmes glared defiantly at Dodd before slipping through the narrow hatchway.

Throughout the twenty minutes or so that Holmes was below the three of us stood smoking in an embarrassed silence. I walked over to the furthest handrail and paused for a moment to speculate upon the mysteries that Holmes expected to solve merely by examination. I gazed across the dark brooding river that was heaving with mercantile traffic, bringing to our doorstep all the fruits of the Empire. The skies above were as murky as the waters beneath, overcast by the incessant discharge from a thousand poisonous chimneys and funnels.

The *Matilda Briggs* would have been partly responsible for this, being a product of the transition from sail to steam. She was quite small for her class, probably no more than 150 feet in length, and had undoubtedly been built for speed. We subsequently discovered that she had been launched in 1874 specifically to deliver tea from the Indies in as few days as possible. Therefore she had been fitted with two full rigs of sail, one at each end of the deck, together with two incongruous funnels in mid-deck which rendered her the most absurdly ugly craft that I had ever seen.

Now, of course a heavy shroud of sadness hung over her. The all-pervading silence of her empty decks was accentuated by the sound of the gentle wash playing on her bows as an endless stream of blackened barges churned their way along the river. The tightly furled rigs reminded me of a grove of lifeless trees in the midst of a harsh winter and all the while I pulled on my collar, although now I was chilled at the thought of the awful tragedy that had recently taken place here and the ultimate fate of all those poor souls who had served on board.

The grating pomposity of Dodd's voice broke in upon my thoughts.

'Well, I must say!' he began, between one of his frequent examinations of his elaborate gold pocket watch. 'I have an appointment in the city to attend, of far greater significance than this, for which I cannot be delayed. Doctor Watson, I should be glad if you would advise your colleague that I shall expect a report of some tangible progress before the week is out.' With that, one last twist of his ridiculous moustache and a most disdainful doffing of his hat, this singularly disagreeable man took his leave.

Of course, his dramatic exit would have carried far greater gravitas and dignity had he experienced less difficulty in negotiating the gangplank down to the small pier. As it was he gingerly edged his way down at a painfully slow pace, guiding each step with his gold-tipped cane. On one occasion he completely lost his footing; he turned round towards us and Lestrade and I realized his worst fears by laughing heartily in his direction. He turned sharply away and completed the remainder of his hazardous departure unscathed. A smart brougham was patiently awaiting him at the quayside and that was the last we saw of Mr Alistair Dodd.

At that precise moment Holmes emerged through the hatchway. He pointed in the direction of the rapidly departing brougham.

'That, I take it, is our esteemed client,' Homes declared.

'Have a care, Holmes,' I warned. 'For all of his absurdities, should Mr Dodd ever decide to withdraw his commission, I am certain that he has enough influence to render any further investigation on our part difficult in the extreme.'

Holmes lit a cigarette and smiled mischievously through its thin, blue plume of smoke.

'The doctor does have a point, Mr Holmes. Has your examination of the ship yielded any clues that might have escaped my men and me?' Lestrade asked, almost as if he was hopeful of a negative reply.

For an instant Holmes appeared to be strangely surprised at the question.

'Well, I suppose there are probably only three of any real note, although to evaluate their significance at this early stage would, of course, be purely speculative,' Holmes quietly replied.

'Three!!' Lestrade squealed, whilst distorting his weaselly features into a mixture of rage and frustration. 'Well, I find that very difficult to believe. My men and I surveyed the craft most thoroughly,' the inspector insisted.

'That is as maybe, but as Watson will certainly attest, I have long insisted that most men have only the ability to see, without making a worthwhile observation. It is the equivalent of reading a great book whilst lacking the power of comprehension. It is a futile waste of time and energy!' Holmes concluded.

'Surely Holmes, you can divulge to us the path that these three clues might be leading us upon?' I suggested hopefully.

'Now, Lestrade, perhaps you would kindly furnish Watson

with the name and address of the shipping line that owns the *Matilda Briggs*. My day's work is by no means complete.' Ignoring my last request, Holmes now glided along the gangplank, down to our waiting cab while Lestrade scribbled a brief note for me as we followed in Holmes's wake.

Once again I was left to marvel at the inexhaustible energy with which Holmes was imbued whenever a new quest was drawing him onwards. Whatever the nature of the ship's mysterious clues they must surely have been of great import to galvanize Holmes in such a fashion. By the time that I had reached the cab, Holmes was already into his pipe and he left it to me to pass the address up to our driver. We had agreed to liaise with Lestrade at every opportunity, and a moment later Holmes and I were on our way to the offices of the Red Cannon shipping line, situated in Pepys Street, close to the Monument.

The density of the traffic rendered the relatively short journey to Pepys Street much longer than it might otherwise have been and at times the narrow streets and lanes were almost impassable. Yet, throughout the entirety of that tiresome journey, Holmes would not be drawn from his self-imposed silence. Therefore I was somewhat relieved when the interminable drive drew at last to a close in one of those tiny side streets that lead down from the Monument to the river's edge. In truth, Pepys Street was little more than a cobbled alley, so it was all the more surprising to find the imposing red-brick headquarters of the Red Cannon shipping line in such a location. I then realized, of course, that the entire neighbourhood was peppered with similar businesses.

I was pondering upon how appropriate it was that the esteemed chronicler had a street named after him so close in proximity to the monument that marked the scene of the subject of some of the best-known entries in his Diaries, the Great Fire. As I was airing these thoughts to Holmes, he suddenly grabbed me by my sleeve and almost wrestled me out of the cab.

'Really Watson, the Great Fire occurred over two hundred years ago! We must remain focused on the current tragedy.' Holmes suddenly moved closer to me and added in a hoarse whisper that was barely audible: 'We must remain alert, for I fear that we have been followed by the cab behind us ... no, do not turn ... from the very moment that we left the wharf!'

We alighted from the cab and, despite the intensity of Holmes's warning as he hustled me discreetly towards the portals of the Red Cannon building, I must confess to having been unable to resist a furtive glance behind me. I could not be certain, as a mist-shrouded gloom was slowly engulfing the City, however, I did catch a tantalizingly fleeting glimpse of what appeared to be an extremely tall figure in a long, dark cape and cowl disappearing around the corner into Monument Square. I thought it best not to mention this at the time, out of fear of ridicule from Holmes; however the image was to remain with me until this mystery could be resolved.

At the very mention of Holmes's name we were shown at once to the offices of the company secretary, a bluff, genial, American gentlemen who went by the name of Declan McCrory. We found him perched, somewhat uncomfortably I would have thought, with one leg draped across a corner of his large oak desk. An enormous cigar remained unlit in the side of his mouth and somehow it showed no signs of falling out when he offered us the broadest of welcoming smiles. Instead of his hand he proffered a brace of Havanas towards us and these we gratefully accepted.

'I am sure that you will not say no to some coffee.' McCrory stated this as a matter of fact rather than making it an invitation to join him. Holmes and I nodded our agreement to this and in a second McCrory had bounded from his desk to the door, from where he barked out an order for three cups to someone called Ethel. Declan McCrory was evidently a man who was used to giving orders and, of course, having them acted upon immediately.

It was hardly surprising, once we had fully taken in his appearance, for he stood at six feet two at the least, and his build was the personification of his desk, large, broad and solid. He was attired in an unfashionable dark-brown suit and this was set off by a brightly coloured cravat that had been stuffed into an open-necked shirt. This vision of an American pioneer was topped off by a veritable mop of unruly blond hair that was constantly falling awkwardly into the man's eyes and was perfectly matched with a brush moustache that appeared to be its extension.

An extremely thin dark-haired woman arrived with a tray of strong black coffee, which she hurriedly deposited on to McCrory's desk before hustling herself out of the room without a single word being exchanged.

'Gentlemen, you must forgive my provincial lack of etiquette,' McCrory apologized whilst waving us towards two extremely low chairs that were strategically positioned on the visitor's side of the desk. I took to my chair, to enable me to make my notes, whereas Holmes, not normally used to looking up to anyone, declined his and positioned himself by the stone fireplace, which he frequently used as an ashtray for his cigar ash.

I noticed that McCrory's lack of savoir-faire extended to the elaborate gold band on his cigar not being removed and the fact that he was taking down far more of its smoke than was being exhaled. I found mine a heady smoke indeed, whereas Holmes was relishing every draw. McCrory noticed this and he looked at us with a mixed expression of sympathy for me and admiration for Holmes.

'The richness of a fresh, moist Havana is not to everyone's taste,' McCrory genially observed. He indicated that he would not be offended if I prematurely abandoned mine in favour of a cigarette, which I promptly did.

'Mr Holmes and Dr Watson, just how may I be of service?' McCrory offered as he took to his seat behind the desk.

'So you know of us, then?' I asked.

'Why, sure I do!' McCrory replied in his mid-western drawl. 'Ever since you so eloquently reported on the great service that Mr Holmes performed for the 'Gold King', Senator Neil Gibson,[1] Mr Holmes's name now resonates throughout the 'Colonies'.'

'Ha! Resonates indeed!' Holmes exclaimed, although neither McCrory nor I could be certain as to whether Holmes's outburst expressed his amusement at the idea of his name 'resonating' or, rather, his appreciation of McCrory's ironic use of the word 'Colonies'. 'I can assure you that it is quite some time since we last referred to the United States as the "Colonies". Now, excellent as your coffee and cigars undoubtedly are, I am certain that you are aware of the reason behind our being here today.'

'I surely am, Mr Holmes,' McCrory gravely responded. 'I am certain that it is regarding the *Matilda Briggs* affair.'

Whilst tightly closing his eyes to aid his concentration, Holmes gestured to me that I should continue with our enquiries.

'What information can you provide us with that might aid us in our investigation?' I asked as I moistened my pencil.

'As you may have already gathered from my accent, I hail from the mid-western states of America, Wyoming to be precise, cattle country. Therefore I only became involved in maritime affairs relatively late in life when my pappy bought a large haulage fleet that operated off of the east coast. He named the line after the locomotive that he had helped design, and as his health sadly declined I was dispatched to London to operate the East Indies side of our operation, which I wished to expand, despite his misgivings. Although I am not inclined towards your damp and misty climate, in all other respects it is not a decision that I have ever regretted, and our business has continued to grow and prosper, much to my father's surprise and relief.

'I can assure you, gentlemen, that in all of my experience this *Matilda Briggs* business is the most damnable and extraordinary of which I have heard. The loss of an entire crew in such a mysterious circumstance is an occurrence that might carry my poor pappy off to his grave if it is not resolved promptly and without scandal. So, yeah, I will help you in any way that I can.' McCrory resoundingly confirmed this by thumping his huge fist down upon the top of his desk.

'I am glad to hear you say so,' Holmes responded, slowly opening his eyes. 'However, the likelihood of this matter being resolved without the generation of scandal is remote in the extreme.'

'Are there any items in the ship's manifest that might indicate the cause of such a tragedy?' I asked.

'I am certain that you already know that the captain's log has mysteriously disappeared. However, the manifest is safely held in these offices and a list of the names of the crew are held by the harbour master. I can provide you with both of these; however, I can assure you that every name upon the list is well-known to us and each one had many years of service behind him, before the mast. The ship's master, Captain James R. Handley, has served the line faithfully for nigh on twenty years, and as he has risen through the ranks his reputation for loyalty and fairness has steadily increased. As for the cargo, well, I am afraid that it was nothing more exotic than Assam tea.' McCrory's voice tailed off as he realized that, so far, he had not imparted anything that would help or enlighten us in our quest.

'Was the recently deceased cabin boy well-known to you?' Holmes asked, moving away from the fireplace and now replacing his cigar with a cigarette.

'No, he was taken on at Port Said on the outward journey,' McCrory replied hesitantly.

'Do you not find it somewhat suggestive that the only crew member with whom you were not familiar was also the only one found alive on board, albeit for just a short while, when the

Matilda Briggs eventually docked?' Holmes stared intently into McCrory's bright, green eyes as if he was boring his way through to the truth.

'Gee no! Hell, he was little more than a boy. Hey, what are you proposing, anyway? That he did away with the remainder of the crew?' McCrory asked, appearing to be somewhat aghast at Holmes's line of questioning.

'At this stage I am not proposing anything, Mr McCrory. You are certain that tea was the only cargo on board?'

'Well of course I am.' McCrory raised his eyebrows, evidently as surprised as I was at Holmes's curious enquiry. 'The *Matilda Briggs*, by virtue of her possessing steam as well as sail, is one of the fastest clippers in our fleet and speed is essential in the carrying of tea.'

'Really,' Holmes said quietly. He turned away while dreamily rubbing his sharp chin with the outside of his right hand. 'You will be able to furnish us with an exact map of the *Matilda Briggs's* entire voyage?'

'Sure, I will have it prepared for you along with the manifest,' McCrory confirmed

'Then I shall take up no more of your valuable time. Come, Watson!' Before I was even able to gather my things together and offer our thanks to McCrory for his hospitality and co-operation, Holmes had turned on his heel and was gone. I was forced to wait for a few moments while Ethel bound together the promised papers before I joined Holmes at the waiting cab.

'You will, no doubt, have noticed that the cab of our pursuers has vanished. They have given up the chase … for now,' Holmes observed with an edge of menace to his voice. He rattled on the cab roof to indicate that we were now ready to depart. As we pulled away I took a furtive glance to see if I could confirm my earlier fleeting vision of a caped stranger at the corner of Pepys Street. I soon dismissed such thoughts as mere flights of fancy.

My past experiences meant that I knew, only too well, of

Holmes's reluctance to divulge his innermost thoughts at this early stage of a case. Therefore it was somewhat tentatively that I broached the subject on our way back to Baker Street.

'You evidently saw far more on board the *Matilda Briggs* than the rest of us,' I quietly commented.

'I saw no more nor less than any of you,' Holmes replied, while a sly, mischievous smile played briefly upon his thin lips. 'However, I observed and, therefore, learnt absolute volumes by comparison!' My blank expression prompted Holmes to continue: 'Oh, Watson, you know my method. Do not bracket yourself with that idiot Lestrade. Deduce!'

I considered my words carefully before offering my response, drawing long and hard from my freshly lit cigarette.

'Based upon your, unusually, insistent line of questioning at the shipping office, I would say that you observed something on board the ship that indicated to you the presence of a cargo other than tea.'

'This is excellent, Watson. Pray continue.'

'Furthermore,' I continued, whilst growing in confidence, 'your request for a sight of the ship's prescribed route would imply that you hope to discover a slight variation from this route and that this might account for the rogue cargo. In all probability the carvings on the deck will help to provide you with a clue as to this variation.'

Holmes clapped his hands gleefully.

'Well, Watson, it would seem that the power to deduce is a most contagious condition. In the future I must be careful not to reveal all of the mysteries of my method!'

I had hoped that this line of conversation would draw Holmes out still further in divulging his other thoughts on the matter of the *Matilda Briggs* and her mysterious secrets. However, I was soon disappointed to learn that, for now at least, he was to remain as enigmatic as ever.

I was pleased to note that we were returning to Baker Street in time for some supper. However, as we were crossing the threshold into 221B, Holmes was alerted to a presence upstairs by an extraordinarily large set of muddied footprints that had been set into the door mat. We were further astonished to note the absence of Mrs Hudson's customary greeting.

Consequently, it was with great stealth and in absolute silence that we ascended the seventeen steps to our rooms. We arrived on the landing without having disturbed the intruder and then crept over to our door. Holmes cautioned me while he strained to hear any sound that might have indicated the intruder's where-abouts within the room. Then he reversed his cane so that the loaded brass handle was now raised and poised to strike.

We were both only too well aware of a chronic squeak in one of the door hinges, so it was imperative that we open the door with fluidity and speed. I am certain that Holmes was more embar-rassed than relieved when he found himself with his cane held menacingly above his head, over nothing more dangerous than our landlady serving tea to an amiable-looking young man, who was perched on the edge of one of our chairs.

It was with a look of startled amusement that Mrs Hudson glanced up towards her illustrious lodger.

'Oh, Mr Holmes, I hope that you do not mind me serving tea to your most patient and charming young visitor. After all, I am sure that he has brought something of interest to you.'

Holmes laughed aloud as he hurriedly stowed away his cane. 'Watson, I say again, the power of deduction does, indeed, appear to be most contagious! On this occasion I believe that Mrs Hudson is certainly correct. Anyone who has awaited us for this period of time must have something more than commonplace to present to us.'

'Mr Holmes,' Mrs Hudson ventured as she prepared to leave with her empty tray. 'If you have only just returned how can you possibly confirm the length of the young man's wait?'

'I am certain of this for I know, only too well, of your meticulous attention to housekeeping. I am sure that you would never have allowed our ashtrays to remain so full during our long absence. Besides, neither Dr Watson nor I smoke that particular brand of Indian cheroots and certainly not in that great a quantity. You really must calm yourself, young man.' Holmes addressed our guest for the first time.

'Now, Mrs Hudson,' he went on, 'if you could manage one more tray for the good doctor and me I shall endeavour to discover the reason behind our young guest's visit and patience.' With a charming smile Holmes gently guided our landlady from the room.

The young man rose somewhat nervously from his chair and shook Holmes wholeheartedly by the hand. 'Mr Holmes, it is such an honour to meet you, and you, Dr Watson, the excellence of whose chronicles has surely led me to your door.'

'Ha! So it is to Dr Watson and his dubiously embellished literary achievements that I am to be indebted for your visit here today. Well, I must say!' Holmes gleefully exclaimed. 'What little reputation my humble practice might possess would look pretty sorry if all my clients come to me in such a manner. Now please resume your seat, while we await Mrs Hudson.'

With that, Holmes strode over to the mantelpiece, where he collected all the plugs and dottles from his previous day's smokes. He filled his old clay pipe with these. Clearly somewhat abashed by Holmes's display of pique, the poor young fellow shifted around uncomfortably in his chair while Holmes smoked in silence for a moment or two.

'Ah, Mrs Hudson!' Holmes stole stealthily over to the door which he flung open before our startled landlady had a chance to knock. He then closed it again behind her in an equally abrupt manner. 'Would you mind, Watson?' Holmes requested whilst waving towards the tea tray.

As I filled our cups I noticed that Holmes was carefully observing our guest. He was certainly newly arrived from the country, for he sported a green tweed hacking-jacket with matching trousers and a pair of dark-brown brogues. However, it was his headwear that caught my attention, for the hat that sat beside him on the arm of his chair, was an absurdly large, floppy felt thing, fashioned in a striking shade of Lincoln green. Holmes stared at our eccentrically attired young guest with an amused intensity, as though he was deciding whether he was to be taken seriously. When Holmes next spoke, his gaze was still upon him and it was not hard to see why.

The young man bore an uncanny resemblance to a young, although undoubtedly Bohemian, Sherlock Holmes! Although his features were not as sharply defined as those of Holmes, they were just as long and inquisitive. The two stood at exactly the same height, were equally slim, and when the fellow crossed his legs, which he did with remarkable frequency, it was with the same slow, languid movement as that employed by my friend.

'So you are an archaeologist, very recently returned from the wilds of Cornwall, I perceive!' Holmes boldly declared.

'Well, I must say, Mr Holmes, that I do not agree with your appraisal of Dr Watson's chronicles if that last statement of yours is anything to go by. You are correct on both counts; however I realize that I have kept you both at a disadvantage. I am Daniel Collier, the only son of the renowned explorer and theologian, Sir Michael Collier.'

'I can assure you, Mr Collier, that my simple observations were merely theatrical examples of the real thoroughness of my method. I should point out that the prints that you left behind on our entrance mat, together with the dry ground in traces on your left knee are unmistakably of the sort of clay found only in our most westerly county. When I then observe red indented calluses set between your right thumb and forefinger, I deduced the constant use of a type of trowel employed by historians in the field. Your attire indicates that you have only recently returned to London, probably today and therefore your mission is of the very greatest moment.

'I repeat, Mr Collier, that I have merely employed pure, elementary logic. However, a somewhat prominent package that I can see struggling to free itself from the inside of your jacket pocket seems to suggest that you are about to test my supposed powers to a far greater extent than I have so far demonstrated.' With that Holmes returned to the Persian slipper for some more tobacco.

'I cannot deny that the content of the package is the reason for my visit here today. However, it contains nothing less than the most recent report of my father's latest set of adventures and it may well prove to be the last! Although as to whether that truly is the case is a matter upon which I crave your help and advice,' Collier implored.

Sensing Collier's intense agitation Holmes immediately responded. 'I can assure you that you are very welcome to both.'

'Bless you for that, Mr Holmes.' Collier breathed in deeply for a moment or two and he appeared to be greatly relieved. 'Despite its great length and detail it might be best if I were to read it aloud to you, if that is agreeable to you?' Holmes nodded his emphatic assent. 'However, before I begin perhaps it would be best if I were to briefly describe my own current circumstances and how things stand between me and the remainder of my family. If I might crave your indulgence for a moment or two ...' Collier pointed towards the open window from where he drew in some welcome fresh air before resuming his craving for Indian cheroots. Repeatedly he ran his fingers through his long flaxen hair before withdrawing a battered brown package from his inside jacket pocket.

Collier then resumed his seat and began speaking in a hushed, reverent tone.

'Sadly, my dear late mother contracted the disease malaria

when she accompanied my father upon his vain quest to establish the authenticity of the Biblical reference to the land of Sheba and its supposed location in North East Africa. Her subsequent untimely passing had a profound and debilitating effect upon my father, who then withdrew to his retreat in Buckinghamshire from where he has only recently emerged.'

'Ah, I had wondered why so little has been heard from him of late,' I interrupted.

Holmes and Collier both turned quizzically towards me. 'Then you already know of my father?' Collier asked.

'Indeed I do!' I confirmed emphatically while rising from my chair. I went across to my small library and from there, adjacent to my prized copy of General Gordon's biography, I extracted a copy of *Journeys Through the Lands of the Bible* by Sir Michael Collier. I displayed this to the author's son by way of confirming my interest in his father's work.

Collier smiled proudly. 'It was certainly one of the expeditions with which he was most gratified.'

'Thank you, Watson,' Holmes murmured. Collier immediately handed the volume back to me, as conscious as I had been of Holmes's irritation at my diversion. Holmes gestured for Collier to resume his story by way of a dramatic wave of his hand. I returned to my seat with my notebook and pencil at the ready.

'Gentlemen, although it might sound absurd for me to say this, under the present circumstances, but my family are extremely close in all respects other than the geographical. Indeed, ever since the tragic passing of my mother all the more so. My beautiful young sister, Charlotte is, at present, engaged in missionary work somewhere in the depths of central Africa. My father is possibly lost somewhere in the East Indies and I have just returned from my study of the mysterious 'Waiting Stones' of Cornwall. The wanderlust has certainly invaded our family and yet wherever it might lead us, we have always felt joined by a common familial bond that shall never be broken ... not even in death.' Collier paused for a moment to put a flame to his cheroot.

'I am familiar with those remarkable standing stones myself. During a recuperative sabbatical on the Cornish coast that very nearly cost me my life,[2] I spent many an hour walking amongst those stones, although I was never able to unlock their ancient secrets,' Holmes observed reflectively during the brief pause. Collier gravely nodded his acknowledgement before continuing:

'Therefore the abrupt ending to my father's most recent letter is all the more surprising. It has been months since he left his retreat to begin his quest to prove that an advanced Hindu civilization had existed long before the period that has been generally accepted by the scholars. He sent me a brief note to the effect that it was his intention to take up the trail of an aged guru whom he had encountered in East Africa and accordingly to sail to Calcutta on the first available schooner from London.

'That was the last that I was to hear from him until this arrived at my lodgings in St Ives, just two days ago.' With that Collier extracted the contents of the envelope that had been the focal point of our attention since we had returned to our rooms. So intent was Holmes on examining the envelope before Collier would have a chance to read its contents that he leapt forward and snatched it from the bewildered young man's grasp. With the same urgency and intent, he held it beside the illumination of a small oil lamp and painstakingly scrutinized every inch of the envelope's surface with his small magnifying glass.

It was only then that I became conscious of the gathering gloom outside our windows. When Mrs Hudson came in to draw our blinds and kindle the fire, I realized that a long though enthralling night lay ahead of us.

CHAPTER FOUR

A Father's Tale

'M r Collier,' Holmes began accusingly, 'why have you retained only one of the envelopes that enclosed these papers?'

'The first was sufficiently large to contain all of my father's correspondence, so therefore the others appeared to be redundant. However, I have not mentioned the fact that there were more than one letter,' Collier explained.

'You did not need to. See here …' Holmes moved over to Collier and then to me, with his glass trained on the seams of the envelope. 'When the envelope was originally sealed the flap folded smoothly over the contents and yet the seams of the bottom two corners are now clearly stretched, almost to the point of splitting in two. This shows something bulkier has been inserted since it was opened. One can sometimes learn more from an apparently unremarkable envelope than from the letter within. Although I am sure that that is not the case in this instance. How many letters are there?'

'There were three in total,' Collier quietly replied, obviously still enthralled by Holmes's simple process of deduction.

'Since I have already deduced that the first of these was the briefest and as it bears a London postmark, it must contain items of a personal nature. Therefore, the other two must provide detailed journals of your father's travels. The stationery and ink are of the highest quality, as one would expect of a man of letters, and the script is strong and confident. May I have a sight of the actual letters before I ask you to read from them?'

'Certainly.' Collier placed them into the clutches of Holmes's eager, outstretched fingers.

Holmes studied the letters with a brief intensity before returning them to our young client.

'Watson, kindly note the fact that the writing employed in each of the letters sadly reflects the fluctuations in Collier's state of mind and his circumstances, as his journeys progressed. The first is written in a strong, bold steady hand, probably in the man's study. The second is written in a similar hand, although its fluctuations indicate the motions of the vessels in which he travelled, and the same stationery and ink are in use. However, the third, truncated, missive is an altogether different affair.

'The writing is now an erratic scratching. The stationery comprises various types of coarse Indian paper and the ink is weak and watery. The fact that it ends abruptly and in mid sentence is most suggestive and is, therefore, of the most concern. Now, I must charge you to omit not a word nor any nuance as you read from each letter in turn.'

Holmes sat crossed kneed upon his favourite chair. His pipe was nestled in the ashtray closest to him while his tightly closed eyes aided his deepest concentration.

Daniel Collier read aloud with a clear, steady and most expressive voice, as if he was reciting from a piece of prose. 'The first letter is dated the fourteenth of July, 1897.'

'Why, that is fully thirteen months ago!' I offered and I observed a brief condescending smile playing over Holmes's thin lips, although his eyes remained tightly shut as he listened to the reading.

My dear boy, I owe you a thousand apologies for having maintained my silence for so long a period of time. I can assure you that this has not been a deliberate attempt of mine to exclude you from my life and my thoughts. Quite the contrary in fact, for not a day has passed without you and our beloved Charlotte having been uppermost in my dreams and in my prayers. Knowing all too well the caring nature of both you and your sister, I can only imagine the pain and anxiety that I have caused you. I have written, in similar fashion, to sweet Charlotte (although heaven only knows if she will ever receive the letter in the depths of Central Africa) and I pray that she will grant me the same forgiveness that I now crave from you.

You must try to understand that the loss of your beloved mother has cleaved a mighty chasm in my life that will never be filled nor healed. A dark, voluminous cloud now hangs over me that no wind will ever disperse. Therefore I have barricaded myself within the confines of our pretentiously titled pile of 'Nirvana' surrounded by my writings and the treasures that I have collected from around the globe. It is only now that I have come to the realization that the only one of these that ever really mattered is the one that can never be restored to me, my dear, sweet wife.

When I remember all the sacrifices that she made in order to satisfy my obsessions and the hardships that she endured, just to be with me throughout my long and perilous journeys, I finally concluded that my self-imposed exile from the world was the last thing that she would have wanted of me.

After all, one lesson that I should have learned from the many books that I have read of the Eastern sages, is that attachment for any thing or any one, is the worst and potentially most dangerous of all of our human failings. Attachment for an idea leads to longing, then to craving and obsession. Attachment for an object and more especially a person leads to pain upon their being lost to you. This pain leads to anger and resentment, hatred and ultimately to loss of intelligence. This is the sorry state that I have descended to of late.

As a consequence I have decided to, once again, take up the trail that I was first led upon by various ancient Sadhus, or holy men, whom I had encountered during my last trip to the Far East. As you might recall it was my intention to examine more closely the notion that an advanced civilization existed in the sub-continent long before the date established by Western historians. Of course, the potential dangers of confirming this most radical of truths had occurred to me and, as your mother was with me at the time, this and the extreme climate that we were experiencing, forced me to abandon the expedition prematurely and return your mother safely to these shores.

Ironically I deemed that the search for Sheba would prove to be a far safer option for your mother to undertake with me. That decision and its tragic consequence, is one that I shall forever regret. So now, in honour of her memory, I shall return to the very cradle of civilization.

Those pious and ascetic Sadhus spoke of a gigantic pillar that had been constructed from an unidentifiable metal. It has neither aged nor corroded throughout its existence. Its age has only recently been calculated by the interpretation of the inscription engraved upon the pillar's circumference. It has been engraved in the ancient form of Sanskrit, the Gupta script. Amongst other things the inscription bears testament to the fact that the pillar was dedicated to the great Hindu god Vishnu by the legendary king, Chandragupta II of the Gupta dynasty. Astoundingly, recent research has proved that he reigned between the years 375-413 A.D! Obviously, therefore, the metal pillar must have been constructed sometime between the fourth and fifth centuries.

I decided that I had to view this astounding relic with my own eyes and to see where this might lead me in my quest, the consequences of which I cannot even begin to speculate upon.

Therefore, I have booked myself passage aboard a small Greek schooner, the *Diomedes* that sails from London on 28 September, bound for Calcutta. I have chosen this particular vessel for she will be laying up at the Cape for several days while she takes on supplies, and it may prove to be an opportunity for me to visit Natal and enquire after news of your sister in the hinterland.

Whether or not I am successful in this I assure you that I shall write to you at every opportunity with news of my progress and well-being. I trust that this remains of interest to you and that my years of absence have not induced indifference. Should God grant me a safe return I will endeavour to heal any resentment that you might bear towards me and to be the father that, perhaps, I always should have been.

'He signs off simply with his initials,' Daniel Collier breathlessly concluded.

'What a remarkably honest and heartfelt insight into a man's regrets and his very soul. We must thank you for allowing us to share it with you,' I said quietly.

Holmes reacted as if my words had broken a spell and he had been awakened from a deep trance. He leapt from his chair and immediately lit a cigarette with the glow from one of our fire's dying embers. He smoked in silence for a moment or two, then glanced at the clock.

'Look at the hour!' he exclaimed. 'I have been most neglectful, Mr Collier. We must refresh you before expecting you to read still further. Watson, you must use your charms, with the fairer sex, and secure for us a tray or two of supper from Mrs Hudson.' This request from Holmes was as surprising as it was welcome and I embarked upon my simple mission with understandable enthusiasm.

When I made my triumphant return, with news of soup and

braised kidneys, Collier excused himself so that he could clear his head with a brisk walk down Baker Street.

'Holmes, I have noted, down the years, how you have always demanded precision and brevity from your clients when they have been outlining their cases to you. Yet in the case of Daniel Collier and his father's remarkable letter, you appear to have hung upon his every word with great intensity and without the impatience that you normally fail to conceal,' I observed quietly while we awaited both our supper and the return of our client.

Holmes observed me quizzically for a moment or two while he lit his cherry-wood. 'Sometimes it is as important to have an insight into the character of the principal in a case as it is to be in possession of the relevant facts. In this instance we are fortunate indeed, for Sir Michael Collier has laid himself bare before us and revealed a remarkable nature. Besides which, I am already convinced that we are about to delve into areas that are considerably beyond the realms of my usual investigations. Therefore, it is impossible, at this early stage, for me to distinguish between those facts that are irrelevant and the ones that might guide us to the truth.'

'You have already heard something that so convinces you?' I asked incredulously.

Holmes smiled enigmatically, as he drew leisurely on his pipe. 'Something suggestive, perhaps,' he stated simply. Unfortunately I was to learn nothing more of my friend's thoughts at this time, for a moment later the welcome sight of Mrs Hudson, awkwardly bearing a heavily laden tray full of food, interrupted us. Daniel Collier returned from his constitutional a moment later and the three of us made short work of our impromptu meal.

Once our empty plates had been cleared away, a glass of port had been poured for each of us and our cigars were under way, we three returned to our seats by the fire and Holmes invited our client to read from his father's second letter. After a long draw

from his cheroot and a sip from his port, the young archaeologist
cleared his throat and began to read.

'The envelope is post-marked Calcutta and the letter itself is
dated the fifteenth of October 1897.

My dearest son Daniel, I sincerely hope that this letter, from the
'Jewel in the Crown' finds you in good health and that your own
investigations are progressing as well as you would have hoped for.

After my last communication I lost little time in securing my
passage aboard the *Diomedes* and I sent my luggage and equipment ahead of me to the port of London, while I closed up and
made arrangements for the house. The *Diomedes* turned out to be
a somewhat smaller vessel than had been originally described to
me and I was disappointed to discover that my berth was barely
large enough to contain my bunk, which itself proved to be far
too small to contain my frame of six feet three inches.

However, the *Diomedes* did have one advantage over the other
available vessels that were departing at this time, in that she was
to lay up in Cape Town for a full three weeks before proceeding
to Calcutta. This fuelled my ambition to travel into Natal in
order to learn more of the ways of the famed Zulu witch
doctors, but, more important, it would give me the opportunity
to make enquiries into the welfare of our sweet Charlotte. This
thought alone consoled me throughout all of my inconveniences
and discomforts.

These were tolerable, at least during the early stages of our
voyage. The glass was set fair, a steady westerly wind filled our
canvas and my treks around the deck were enjoyably bracing. All
this ended somewhat abruptly, however as we edged our way
across the infamous Bay of Biscay.

The wind that had, so far, proved to be our compliant servant,
suddenly turned to a northerly and seemed to unleash its pent-
up frustrations against us as the tempest sought to destroy us.

Our masts were suddenly dwarfed by the unimaginable height of the sheer, white waves that threatened to engulf our tiny vessel. The ship's master, Captain Theo Economides, ordered that every non-essential crew member and passenger be confined below decks and there we were to remain, battened down, for three full days and nights!

I can assure you, my dear boy, that those three days might as well have been three months. My 'cupboard' seemed to shrink with each passing hour and the time between each striking of the bell appeared to get longer and longer. The waves, however would not be denied as they cascaded throughout every crevice of the ship's timbers. Then, to add to our woes, a particularly ferocious lashing drowned and snuffed out the fire in the cook house, thus ensuring that our meagre rations were cold and almost inedible.

I attempted every means that I could devise to shut out our perilous condition from my mind. Then I thought back to the teachings of the very gurus whom I was now on my way to meet once again and the ancient practice of meditation proved to be my salvation. The sounds of the heaving waves were suddenly muted and the rise and fall of the ship slowly levelled off, my hunger became nothing more than a minor inconvenience.

I heard Holmes emit a grunt of approval and admiration as Daniel Collier read out this last paragraph. He held up the palm of his hand in front of the young fellow's face, to temporarily halt his narration, then he proceeded to fill his pipe from the Persian slipper.

'Your father would seem to be both brave and very wise. You must be most proud of his achievements,' Holmes quietly suggested.

'Oh, indeed I am, sir!' Collier agreed enthusiastically. 'The adventures that he is describing here are not unique among the journals of his travels. I have retained every one of them.'

'Yet you never sought to emulate him nor accompany him upon these adventures?'

'Oh, Mr Holmes, although I have inherited his enquiring mind and his fervent interest in ancient religions, my interests are of a more academic bent, and, being in possession of a keen attention for detail, I am certain that my researches into the secrets of the 'Waiting Stones' will fully occupy me for some time to come. Perhaps, one day, I shall take up my father's preoccupations and accompany him to areas further away than Cornwall.'

'Are there no other reasons why you have not yet done so?' Holmes asked this question in a tone that suggested that he already knew the answer before it was asked.

Collier hesitated for a moment before he replied, and when he did so he appeared to be more than just a little bit abashed. 'You are quite right, of course, Mr Holmes. As befits a man of his many talents and achievements, my father is endowed with a somewhat larger-than-life personality. Although I have a deep affection for him and not a little admiration, I do find him overbearing over a period of time, to the extent that I could scarcely imagine being in close proximity to him for what could be months on end. Although I take a keen interest in his discoveries, I try not to let it detract from my own endeavours.'

'Your father does seem to take greats pains in involving you in every aspect of his journey and I thank you for your honesty.' Holmes casually waved his hand to indicate that Collier should now continue reading from his father's second letter.

As we left the Bay behind us the winds dropped dramatically and the *Diomedes* steadied as the waves fell to a tolerable level. Indeed, as we struck out down the west coast of Africa, we saw some warm sunlight and we were soon allowed back on deck.

When we did so the appalling effects of the storm were immediately evident and it was decided that some timber was needed to repair our shattered central mast. Under normal circumstances the remaining masts might have proved sufficient, however several of the remaining sails had been torn asunder and the air pressure had now risen so sharply that we were positively becalmed and making little progress.

Since we were now lying off of the Ivory Coast, Captain Economides decided to dispatch a small landing party to secure the necessary timber, shards of which appeared to line the water's edge in rich abundance. He intended to execute the repairs as we progressed, in order to reduce the inevitable delay to our arrival at the Cape.

And so our sorry craft limped towards the Victoria and Albert docks a full sixty-nine days after our departure from London, drawing sixteen feet of water, still nursing our wounded mast. I congratulated Economides on his steadfast seamanship and then ensured that I was aboard the first dinghy to make for shore.

As you might well imagine, upon disembarking I wasted little time in securing for myself a small, but comfortable room, furnished with a deep bath and plenty of hot water. The revital-izing effect was completed by my consumption of the greater part of a more than acceptable Scotch whisky. I then stretched myself out upon a far larger bed than I had been used to aboard ship, there to remain for a full three days!

Once I was suitably recovered, I lost little time in tracking down my old friend, a former army officer, whom I may have mentioned in my earlier journals, namely Lieutenant Marcus Harrison VC. His large house, set back in the lush hills above the Cape, was not hard to find and a friendly Kaffir who laboured in Harrison's hugely successful livery business, leased me a small trap for a nominal rate.

It was my intention to utilize my time during the period of the refit to the *Diomedes*, by striking out into Natal to see if any news might be gained of Charlotte's mission.

Ever since the defeat of the Zulus on the banks of the sacred River Umvolosi and the subsequent death of their warlike King, Cettiwayo in '84, Zululand has been largely subdued. The occasional insurrection, led by King Divi Zulu, reminded the British of the Zulus' warrior history, however he had been exiled to the island of St Helena, ironically when you consider that Divi Zulu was a direct descendant of Chaka, the 'Black Napoleon'. Last year Zululand was formally incorporated into British Natal.

As a consequence the Zulus have now swapped their lethal assegai[1] for the plough and trowel and an ever increasing army of would-be immigrants are now being actively encouraged to seek their fortune in this newly pacified land. This was where Harrison and his livery came in. The only form of transport that was suitable for these immigrants and their chattels, to travel over this particular terrain, happened to be Harrison's large ox-drawn carts.

Harrison kindly offered me the use of his finest cart and pair and, together with three of his Kaffirs, I struck out to the north on the following morning towards what had once been known as the land of the Zulus! Before too long we were clear of the outskirts of Cape Town and as we headed northward we were at once surrounded by a range of magnificent, undulating hills that rose and fell like gigantic waves.

I must confess to having been unable to suppress an intense thrill of excitement at the thought of fifty thousand assegais[1] crashing against fifty thousand shields and their thunderous roar echoing around the very hills through which I was now travelling. It was a sobering thought that, in the very recent past, the impis[2] of Cettiwayo had prepared to descend upon their doomed victims from these spectacular rolling peaks.

Now, however, the only sound to be heard was the creaking of my cart's wheels and the occasional snort from one of my oxen as they toiled towards the Buffalo River, the former border with

Zululand. Occasionally we came upon a small Zulu farmstead, but the only reminder of their former ferocious legacy would be a decorative cowhide shield hanging over a doorway or a forbidding-looking young man in a leopard-skin robe tending his cattle. All traces of the once influential witch doctors, that I had come so far to see, had all but disappeared as a result of the new regime strictly forbidding the practising of their ancient arts.

However, my priority remained the discovery of news of our Charlotte and in that quest you should be glad to hear I was considerably more successful. I discovered from Lieutenant Harrison that among the more influential missions was the one at Lovedale run by its Scottish Presbyterian principal, the Reverend Joseph Stewart. He was a gruff, though affable gentleman who was most passionate about his work and who genuinely loved the people he was working amongst.

Over a glass of lemonade on his shaded veranda, Stewart explained to me how it was that Lovedale's very success had prompted Charlotte to move ever northward, into Matabeleland, where she felt that her efforts and experience would be put to better use. Indeed the opening of the hospital made her feel redundant and, reluctantly, Stewart gave his blessing to her future endeavours.

Stewart receives regular news of the progress at the new mission and assured me that Charlotte remains in good health and in high spirits. He promised to impart news of my visit to her and I turned my cart towards the Cape once more, with a considerably gladder heart than when I had departed. As it turned out, the day of my return was well-timed, for I arrived at the quayside having had barely sufficient time to gather my belongings from my hotel room. I tumbled aboard the Diomedes only moments before she pushed off.

As soon as I had stowed my gear, I got to the deck in time to see Table Mountain shrinking into the misty distance and I turned my gaze towards the Indian Ocean, which was now spread majestically before me. Ignoring the shaking heads and the Greek mutterings of the crew as they contemplated the 'eccentric Englishman', I remained on deck until the crimson sun had melted into the vast expanse of sea that lay between me and the culmination of my quest.

I was on my way to Calcutta!

Although the letter was by no means near completion, I felt that this was an appropriate juncture to remind my companions that the clock had just announced midnight. Holmes nodded his assent and poured out three cognacs as Collier temporarily folded away his father's epic letter once again.

CHAPTER FIVE

A Journey to the Islands

'Gentlemen,' cried Collier, suddenly jumping up from his chair and still holding his glass of cognac. 'I owe you both a thousand apologies for having occupied so much of your time with my concerns.'

Holmes dismissed these regrets with a wave of his hand and a shake of his head. 'Finish your drink and calm yourself, Mr Collier. Dr Watson and myself have both been known to keep the most bohemian of hours, from time to time,' Holmes assured him.

'Is there someone awaiting you who may be concerned at your continued absence?' I asked.

'No, not at all.' Collier shook his head, as if ashamed at this admission.

'In that case, should you have no obvious objections, it might be best if you were to remain here overnight,' I suggested.

'Watson! I was on the point of proposing the very same thing,' Holmes exclaimed.

'I could not possibly so impose myself,' Collier protested.

'Nonsense. I shall instruct Mrs Hudson to make up my bed for you, and I shall spend the night in here. I shall not brook any further protest. I have spent more nights in my chair than you might reasonably imagine.'

So the matter was settled and as I began climbing the stairs up towards my room, I looked back to see Holmes settling into his favourite chair with an ashtray and a supply of tobacco and vestas by his side.

It was no surprise, to me at any rate, to find Holmes already dressed and fresher than we were as I came down for breakfast on the following morning. He was already at his usual breakfast of coffee and cigarettes, by the time Collier and I finally emerged.

'Bohemian hours indeed!' Holmes laughed as he tossed a half-smoked cigarette into his coffee cup. 'I trust that you will take some of Mrs Hudson's more than adequate breakfast before continuing with your father's remarkable tale.'

Collier nodded his assent and made short work of his grilled kipper and eggs, a meal which I also heartily enjoyed. Holmes viewed us both with some amusement as he lit another cigarette.

As he wiped his plate clean Collier glanced somewhat sheepishly towards Holmes, obviously aware of Holmes's empty plate and untouched cutlery.

'Will you not be joining us, Mr Holmes?'

To save Holmes from the tiresome task of explaining himself I offered an explanation of my own.

'When Mr Holmes is engrossed in a case, especially one as unusual as yours, he finds that the energy expended in the digestive process could be better used in maintaining the sharpness of his mental faculties. Do not let his abstinence detract from your own enjoyment of the meal, for I assure you that Holmes's appetite will return upon the successful conclusion of the matter.'

Holmes clapped his hands together gleefully.

'Well done, Watson!' he exclaimed. 'I could not have expressed the thing better myself. However, engrossing as Mr Collier's letters undoubtedly are, we must not neglect the other matter that has so recently been brought to our attention. I am certain that Lestrade is already being cajoled by the odious Mr Dodd into replacing our services with those of another agency. So, with that in mind, would you stroll to the vendors to procure a copy of *The Times* while I provide Lestrade with a suggestion or two and dispatch Mrs Hudson with a couple of wires that may prove to be significant?'

'Of course, the *Matilda Briggs* affair!' I must admit that the enthralling nature of Sir Michael Collier's tale had occluded any thought of the mysterious ship and our unpleasant client. However, as I went to fetch my coat and carry out Holmes's instruction, the memories of the previous afternoon at the quay-side and at the office of the Red Cannon shipping line came flooding back to me. I craved Collier's indulgence and made for the door as Holmes began scribbling out his notes.

The light mist that I had observed the previous day as it had spread itself lazily across the Thames had thickened substantially overnight. As it merged with the constant discharge from the forest of chimneys that surrounded us, it had transformed into this monstrous, swirling, grey pre-souper that appeared to swallow up all that was in its path.

Even the 'Empty House', that had once been the scene of one of Holmes's investigations and stood opposite to our own lodging became nothing more than a ghostly apparition and any fool-hardy passers-by stole along like so many crouching shadows. I turned up my coat collar and pulled down my hat as I continued upon my mission.

As soon as I had stepped out on to the street I was engulfed by the swirling gloom. Indeed, as I made my way towards the corner with Marylebone Road, I missed my footing several times. I reached the stand of Simon, my usual vendor, without any further mishap and the scarcity of customers that morning prompted me to slip him a few extra loose coins to cheer his gloomy counte-nance. I was on the point of turning for home with my paper under my arm, when the first rays of sunlight began to dissipate the edges of the mustard-tinged fog. I therefore decided to extend my walk, and to while away the time that Holmes would need to put his plans into motion by stretching my stiff legs.

After a hundred yards or so, I decided that I could not trust Holmes's impatient nature for a moment longer; as there was a real possibility he would ask Collier to continue with his reading in my absence. I turned around sharply at the thought and beat a hasty retreat towards 221B. When I reached the crossroads, however, my attention was drawn towards the opposite corner, for there stood, without a doubt, the very caped figure that had so perplexed me in Pepys Street the previous afternoon!

I stood there rubbing my eyes in disbelief and on this occasion I decided to make after the fellow. My previous vision of the man was so fleeting that I had been unsure of what I had witnessed and, consequently, I could not even bring myself to mention it to Holmes. The traffic was infrequent and so, despite my aching leg, I sprinted over to the opposite corner with the intention of confronting our stalker.

I am not normally prone to flights of fancy, but I could swear that this phantom had vanished into thin air by the time that I had reached the corner where the figure had stood but a moment before. I turned round in a circle and ran this way and that, but all to no avail. Despite all of my best efforts and the improved visibility created by the ever strengthening sun, I was forced to concede that the strange apparition was nowhere to be seen!

Eventually I gave up my search and returned to 221B, determined that this second sighting was certainly no mere illusion. I was entirely convinced that the phantom's appearance at two supposedly random locations was by no means coincidence, and I immediately lengthened my stride towards home.

In my excitement I took our stairs two at a time, yet, to my surprise, I was greeted by Holmes at the door to our rooms. He held a cautionary finger before his lips, thereby beseeching me to silence.

'Watson,' Holmes whispered, 'if you have any important news to impart to me, please do so at a later time.' He crooked a discreet finger in the direction of two familiar figures that were seated by the fire.

Sure enough, there was Inspector Lestrade, perched uncomfortably on the edge of his seat with anxiety etched indelibly into his ferret-like features, sitting next to Mr Alistair Dodd, who appeared to be as pompous and pugnacious as he had been on board the *Matilda Briggs* the previous afternoon. They both half-rose by way of a greeting and I nodded briefly in return.

'Good day to you Doctor ... er.' Dodd began.

'Watson!!' I snapped, still feeling frustrated at having to suppress the recounting of my news.

Holmes moved over to the fireplace and began fumbling for some tobacco from the Persian slipper, while young Collier sat patiently in the corner, evidently ready to resume reading from his father's letter. Once Holmes had replaced his lit pipe on the mantel he turned around fiercely to face our guests. With his hands on his hips, a stance that splayed out both vents of his long, black frock-coat most menacingly, he glowered down at them.

'Gentlemen, to what do we owe the dubious pleasure of your company this morning?' Holmes asked of them.

Lestrade merely stammered nervously and it was left to Dodd to state the reason for their visit.

'To be frank then, Mr Holmes, against my better judgement and advice my clients have nonetheless decided that you are the best man to carry out the investigation into the *Matilda Briggs* tragedy on their behalf. I was not at all impressed by your cavalier attitude on board the ship yesterday and your apparent indifference to the seriousness of the situation does not recommend you to me, either.'

'Mr Dodd, I am hardly likely to be apathetic towards a case that promises to be every bit as stimulating as any that have come my way of late,' Holmes disdainfully retorted.

'That is as maybe; however we did not bring this matter before you merely to provide you with some stimulation. We require results and we expect them with as little fuss and within the shortest time as is practicable. Who might this person be?' Dodd asked as he gestured towards Daniel Collier. 'I trust that he is not another client and one who might further distract you from your work.'

'This person just happens to be the son of the renowned explorer and historian, Sir Michael Collier. He is also an old friend of my family,' I indignantly responded.

'Bravo, Watson,' I heard Holmes murmur under his breath. 'Mr Dodd,' Holmes continued in a somewhat louder tone, 'the only person here distracting me from my work is yourself! I have already dispatched two suggestions for the good Inspector's attention and I hope to have a response to a wire within the next forty-eight hours. Now, I do not intend to take up any more of your valuable time, in the same way that I am certain that you do not wish to waste any more of mine!'

With that Holmes turned once more to his pipe and indicated with a gesture that our uninvited guests should make their way to the door without delay. Dodd was on the point of making a further remark, but evidently thought better of the idea. With Lestrade in tow and his face reddened with indignation, Alistair Dodd finally took his leave.

Holmes slapped his hand on the mantel triumphantly and began laughing uproariously.

'Well I never! I fear that if that man's face had turned any redder it would have been in grave danger of exploding. Now, Mr Collier,' Holmes calmed himself with a deep breath or two, 'with a thousand apologies for that unseemly interruption, I would beseech you to continue reading from your father's extraordinary letter.'

'I shall by all means, Mr Holmes, but I should not wish to

divert you from what appears to be a matter of the greatest moment,' Collier replied.

'My dear fellow, do not be dismayed at Mr Dodd's discourteous conduct. Singular though the *Matilda Briggs* affair undoubtedly is, we have already travelled too far with your father to be put off at this stage,' I said encouragingly.

Collier smiled appreciatively as he lit another of his cheroots and looked to Holmes for confirmation. Holmes smiled and nodded his assent while the young archaeologist took up those crumpled sheets once more.

Mercifully, the second leg of our journey was blessed with somewhat less uncomfortable conditions than those that had blighted and almost destroyed the first. We appeared to be skimming rather than cutting through the still shimmering surface of the azure sea, yet even so the constant westerly moved us along at a most favourable rate of knots.

We then sailed across the Bay of Bengal and approached Calcutta through the broad and spectacular expanse of the Ganges delta. By the time we had completed the triangle of Colombo, Madras and Calcutta I had been aboard for the best part of one hundred days and I bade the captain and crew of the *Diomedes* a heartfelt farewell as we all disembarked. When I was halfway down the pier I slowly turned around and viewed the brave, battered hulk that had been my home for so long, with a strange nostalgic fondness. As I turned towards shore once more, I was most grateful to find that a friendly and familiar face was there to greet me.

I am certain that I have previously mentioned to you my guide to the Islamic traditions of India, a devout and most resolute fellow who goes by the name of Mohamed Abdi Mohamed. I could not help but smile as he waved his greeting, for he reminded me of the sun in a human incarnation.

Mohamed was attired in a long, white, gold-edged robe, which was also draped over his head. However, it was his face that was the most striking aspect of his appearance. His neat, tightly curled beard had noticeably whitened since I had last seen him and it encircled the broad expanse of his warm, welcoming smile. Evidently the letter which I had dispatched from the Cape, had reached him safely and had found him available and willing to guide me once again.

He saluted me as his brother and immediately took hold of my baggage as he led me to his family home, which proved to be a short walk from the quayside. The dwelling that he led me to was a small though comfortable, white-walled, square, two-storey building, which was festooned in brightly decorated, hand-made rugs and drapes.

The warmth and hospitality that was shown towards me, a man who was, to all present save for Mohamed, nothing more than a stranger (and an infidel to boot), was overwhelming. Therefore, by the time that I eventually stretched out upon the mat that was made available to me, on the cooling roof-top veranda, I was both full and satisfied.

I am certain that I would have remained asleep until well into the afternoon had it not been for the penetrating call to prayer that resonated from each of the surrounding minarets, which immediately aroused Mohamed and his family. The enthusiasm with which they went about their preparations to depart for the nearest mosque was truly inspiring and I was left in little doubt of their sincerity and devotion.

In their absence I was left to my own devices and as I set out to explore the surrounding neighbourhood I was immediately struck by the levels of poverty and squalor to which the majority of the people were being subjected.

There was little doubt in my mind that the streets I was now walking through were, indeed, the fields wherein the seeds of discontent and revolt against the British Raj were being sown. I decided that much credence should be given to the rumours that were filtering back to Britain; rumours that told of extremists being mobilized under the banner of the Ghadar movement and that dark days, comparable with those of the Indian mutiny were fast approaching once again.

To make matters worse, one of their leaders, Bal Gangadhar Tilak from Maharashfa, had evoked the Hindu Gods Ganesh and Shivaji and he was using their name to rally revolutionists to his banner. Obviously this had led to the British forces being placed on high alert and the tension was now all encompassing. Furthermore, the object of my quest, being of Hindu origin, now took on an altogether more sensitive nature and my journey and enquiries would have to be far more discreet than I had at first allowed for.

I decided to return to Mohamed's home with all speed and immediately unpacked my notes and maps. My intention was to persuade Mohamed to depart with me to Delhi at the earliest practical moment, in the hope that my journey could be concluded before travel restrictions were imposed by the authorities.

Fortunately Mohamed was more than willing and able to comply with my plans and, on the following morning, I went to the station to make the arrangements for the earliest possible departure. Mohamed ensured that there would be sufficient time for him to visit the mosque for one last time before agreeing to such an early train, and we returned home to break the news to his family.

As we arrived at the station I was immediately struck by an all-pervading military presence. The threat of revolt was suspended above the heads of every race, creed and caste throughout the land and nowhere was it more in evidence than within that vestibule of heaving human masses. Our platform alone swarmed with hundreds of would-be passengers and we had serious misgivings of even being able to reach our berth, much less the train departing on time!

Once we had forced our way into a carriage we found that the conditions aboard that veritable sweat-box were intolerable and that the validity of our first class tickets was as nothing. The fourth-class passengers, who would, under normal circumstances, have been condemned to travelling on the train's roof, were now displaced by a line of protective riflemen on top of each car.

By the time we had passed through Bengal and reached Parna, to take on water, every person on board was thoroughly exhausted and used this time in taking refreshing walks around the station perimeter. Mohamed and I lost little time in taking this welcome opportunity and observed that the only people not sharing this relief were the rooftop soldiers.

Then we pressed on through Pudh and the North Western Provinces, where the terrain took on an altogether more striking aspect and our overburdened train suddenly appeared to be quite inadequate and precarious. Every ravine crossing became a most perilous undertaking as the raging torrents growled menacingly beneath us.

More worrying, however, was the increasingly visible presence, on the surrounding hillsides, of Afghan horsemen, who brandished their swords and let up a constant hollering in a most menacing manner. On one occasion the side of the train was lightly peppered by a sporadic volley of Afghan bullets. However, our rooftop cordon of khaki-clad guardians possessed far greater firepower than our would-be assailants, who soon sought the higher ground. Apart from a stray bullet grazing the forehead of an engineer, this threat never became anything more than that and we were able to reach Delhi unscathed.

Such was the size and extent of Mohamed's family that it was no great surprise to find that a first cousin of his lived no more than twenty minutes' walk away from the station.

I can assure you, my dear boy, that only sheer exhaustion had brought about any sleep that night, for I knew that I was now only a short walk away from the culmination of my quest, the bewildering, ancient mosque of Quwwatu'l-Islam Masjid. Fortunately it is also often referred to as the 'Friday Mosque' which will make it far easier for me to refer to!

The poisonous atmosphere of hatred and mistrust that infused the relationships between Moslem, Hindu and Raj rendered my presence at the mosque a potential cause of unrest. Therefore Mohamed decided that it would be wisest if I were to retain the Jilab that he had loaned me for the train journey, and that we two pose as pilgrims intent at worshipping at the Friday Mosque.

As we approached this remarkable edifice, early on the following morning, my first instinct was to begin my examination of the mysterious motifs and inscriptions, with which it was so copiously adorned, without a moment's delay. However, that would not have been the behaviour of a devout pilgrim and so, for now, I suppressed my scholarly enthusiasm by following Mohamed's lead.

He had lent me a prayer mat for this purpose and, once we had spread these out before us, I emulated each and every one of Mohamed's sounds and movements. I ensured, all the while, that my long and unruly flaxen hair and beard remained fully covered, for a sight of these would surely have discredited my guise. Once the morning prayers had been concluded we rolled up the mats once more and Mohamed passed me a gourd of cool refreshing water, for the sun had become most piercing.

Then Mohamed took up a position on the ridge of a small nearby hill, from where he could best warn me of the first signs of unrest or disturbance. He then left me to my own devices and

I attempted to pursue my examinations in as pious a manner as I could manage. I assure you, dear boy, that this was no easy task!

For me to say that the Friday Mosque was an astounding piece of architecture would be to serve its creators no true justice. Thankfully, only Mohamed was aware of my childlike gaping as I gazed up at each new wonder. However, it was only when I began to examine the mosque's pillars that I could confirm that every piece of stone and masonry had been pillaged from the twenty-seven Hindu temples of Qila Rai Pithora, as the pre-Islamic, Hindu motifs attested.

This fact had been recorded by the builder of the mosque, Qutub-ud-Din Aibak, in his beautifully fashioned Islamic inscriptions. However the present religious tensions and my sense of political discretion precluded me from voicing this discovery, even, or perhaps especially, to Mohamed. The mystery of the place, however was the famed iron pillar, set in the centre of the courtyard.

That the mosque was, undoubtedly, constructed in the twelfth century and that the 'iron' pillar itself was identified by its Sanskrit inscription as having been constructed in the fourth century AD are facts that I have already recorded in the early part of my letter. The mystery does not end there, though, for I can now confirm that no other relic of the fourth century exists anywhere else on this extensive site and the pillar's place of origin is unknown!

I approached this elegantly tapered creation with understandable reverence. It stood at well over twenty feet in height, with a further three feet embedded below its wrought-iron knobbly foundations. Although this section is showing minimal signs of deterioration it is, nonetheless, a sobering thought to consider that those ancient Indian metallurgists were producing an indestructible, pure malleable iron, at a time in history when their modern day rulers were living in mud huts and painting their bodies in blue!

My examination of the inscriptions around its circumference confirmed its builder as being Chandragupta II, and also showed that an empty hole at the pillar's fine peak, told of a missing arte-fact, the discovery of which could, potentially, have far-reaching political significance. I decided, there and then, that it was my duty to trace this artefact's whereabouts and to prevent it from falling into dangerous hands.

Regretfully, I soon realized that the longer I continued with my examination the more likely it was that I would soon attract some unwanted attention. However, when I looked up at the hilltop, from where Mohamed was supposed to have been keeping watch, to my horror there was no sign of my friend! At once I abandoned the pillar and looked about me in every direc-tion to see if my guide and sentinel was anywhere to be found. Under the circumstances, I walked as calmly and unobtrusively as I could, until I had reached the summit of Mohamed's hill.

I was on the point of despair when a familiar, full, booming laugh echoed from behind me. Mohamed was evidently amused by the look of anxiety on my face, as nothing more sinister had happened to him than the call to prayer. He waved his prayer mat above his head by way of explanation, and advised me to return with him to his cousin's house without delay. This was advice that I followed without any hesitation, for I decided that I was becoming a dangerous companion for Mohamed to be seen with.

The following morning Mohamed returned to Calcutta and we bade each other what would, in all probability, be our final farewell. Once I was assured that he had safely made his train, I set about putting my own plans into action. The return journey to Calcutta was now too long and risky for me to undertake and an examination of my maps showed that the significantly shorter land journey to the Bay of Cambay could prove to be a far safer option.

It was now my intention to discover the whereabouts of the very same Sadhu who had set me upon my quest to the 'iron' pillar in the first place. He had last been heard of living in a cave just outside a small village near Madras, which was certainly reachable by sea from Cambay. Therefore, the way ahead for me was clear.

As it happened I was able to find the Sadhu, Kiran Mistry, with considerably less difficulty than I had at first expected. His name and reputation had spread wide from his hilltop cave, and the streets of Madras were positively ringing with his name. Finding him and gaining access to his presence proved to be two entirely different propositions, however, and I was forced to wait a full forty-eight hours before he was able to beckon me to his side.

That he was a devotee of Shiva was identified by his entire body being caked in a dry crust of grey ash. He sat in the middle of a small circle of his disciples. His frail body was weighed down by countless rosary-bead strands that rattled resonantly with his every movement. Mistry and his disciples were passing round a large cigar, which, I subsequently discovered, was rolled from charas, more commonly known by its Arabic name of hashish, a plant from Nepal that apparently aided the Sadhu's spiritual and mental clarity when it was smoked. I must confess that the effect that it had on me was quite the opposite and my entire experience was overwhelming.

Once we were alone I was able to speak to him, at some length, of my life since our last meeting and for the first time I found that I could discuss the loss of your dear mother without feeling pain. He smiled fondly upon me when I told him of this and before long we were discussing the reason behind my being in Madras. To my astonishment the Sadhu knew precisely of the artefact I was seeking, although he would not have approved of the political significance that I had attached to it.

Mistry spoke of an elegantly curved ceremonial blade, known as a beladau, which, to his knowledge, was the only object in existence to have been crafted from the same 'iron' as had been the pillar of Delhi. Mistry, of course, spoke of its spiritual value and significance whereas its political significance seemed to be of the utmost importance.

However, my worst fears were soon realized when the Sadhu revealed that the beladau had last been seen in the hands of the aforementioned revolutionary leader, Bal Gangadhar Tilat as he invoked Shiva at a recent rally. Apparently, after the rally had been broken up and dispersed by a line of British infantrymen, a splinter group of the Ghadar movement had fled with the beladau to the Dutch stronghold of Aceh, in northern Sumatra, where they could then regroup following the arrest of Tilat.

The dangerous significance of this situation was not lost upon me. After all, should it have been proved that the beladau was as ancient as it was thought to be, then it would further weaken the British dominance over the people of the Indian colonies who had fashioned this object in the age of antiquity. It fell to me, I reasoned, the only person in possession of all the facts, to reclaim the beladau before the Ghadar, or even the Dutch, could realize the beladau's destructive potential.

I thanked Mistry for his guidance and for his blessings and immediately chartered a small fishing boat to take me back to Calcutta. For three days and nights I waited in vain for news of available transport to Sumatra. The war between the Dutch and the Sultanate of Aceh, over the control of one the most important and affluent ports in the whole of the Far East, had flared up again. This conflict had been raging sporadically for nigh on thirty years and on this occasion the fighting had been most fierce and had resulted in a significant loss of life.

Understandably enough, there was not a captain in the whole port at Calcutta willing to undertake so perilous a journey, no matter how potentially profitable the cargo might be. Therefore I would have to approach Sumatra by way of a far more tortuous route. I learned of a supply vessel that was scheduled to take post and medicine to the troops manning the British penal colony at Port Blair, on the Andaman Islands. From there—

'Holmes!' I blurted out suddenly. 'The Andaman Islands! Surely that was the homeland of that ghastly and deadly little creature, Tonga.' Captivated as I undoubtedly had been by every one of Collier's words, I now found it impossible to contain myself at the mere mention of the land that had spawned the tale of the 'Sign of Four'.[1]

'Yes, Watson.' Holmes smiled condescendingly at me. 'Well, in any event, your excitable interruption at least affords me the opportunity to replenish my pipe and to send downstairs for a most welcome tray of tea.' Holmes uncoiled himself from his chair and sprang up towards his Persian slipper.

'My dear young sir,' I said quietly by way of an apology as I made my way to the door to summon Mrs Hudson.

'Do not trouble yourself, Dr Watson,' Daniel Collier courteously responded. 'Besides, as you might have noticed by the increasing hesitation in my reading, the last page or so has been scribed in a far thinner ink than that employed hitherto by my father. This and my father's faltering script, has placed a strain upon my eyes that might well be alleviated by a few minutes' break and perhaps a brief refreshing walk.'

'By all means!' I exclaimed, relieved at having my rudeness so graciously dismissed.

While Collier went to fetch his coat and his strange headwear, Holmes indicated to me that this might be an opportune moment to recount the information that I had been harbouring ever since my return from my mission to the Marylebone Road.

Having satisfied myself that our street door had been securely closed behind Daniel Collier, I lit a cigarette and told Holmes of everything that I had observed at the corner of Pepys Street on the previous afternoon and all of what had occurred when I had gone to fetch the papers, after breakfast on that very morning.

Knowing full well of Holmes's requirement for precise and accurate details, there was not one element of my strange encounters that I had omitted. I must confess that I had been quite looking forward to seeing the look of astonishment upon Holmes's face once I had completed my narration. However, I was to be disappointed, for when I glanced towards him I realized that his expression had not changed!

I glared at Holmes somewhat aggrievedly.

'You do not appear to be as surprised at what I have just told you as I might reasonably have expected.'

Holmes turned rather sheepishly away from me before returning my glare.

'Watson, I will not insult your intelligence by claiming that I had expected this startling turn of events. Equally, however and with due honesty, I must say that I am not entirely surprised either. I would also say that I should be most surprised if you were to report that this 'phantom' of yours were not sporting a large pair of straw sandals upon his feet.'

'He was!' I exclaimed loudly, completely taken aback at his accuracy. 'You are evidently in possession of far more information than you have, so far, revealed to me,' I added with justifiable disappointment.

'That is as maybe, Watson, but you surely know me better than any other man alive. So when I tell you that, although certain elements are falling very nicely into place, our puzzle is far from completion; you should know this to be the entire and absolute truth. I am in little doubt that our mysterious stalker is a man, every inch as solid as either you or I. There is certainly nothing spectral about him and I am convinced that he will prove to be a most accomplished and dangerous individual.'

'Good heavens! You consider him to be a threat, then?'

The look on Holmes's face visibly darkened and his voice dropped to a hoarse whisper before he spoke again.

'Oh, indeed I do, my dear fellow, and not only to ourselves, I fear. Our stalker seems to be keeping us under a very close surveillance. Therefore I am afraid we have to assume he is very much aware of the presence of Daniel Collier and our recent association with him. His life is under threat as surely as ours are.

'In this new set of circumstances, I think that it might be prudent if you were to interrupt his constitutional and invite him to conclude his father's tale without a moment's more delay!'

Holmes dismissed me with a cursory wave while he took up a position by the window. I almost collided with Mrs Hudson, who was arriving with our tea, as I hurried off to achieve my mission. However and to my intense relief, young Collier was already arriving back at our door at the very moment that I was flinging it open. I ushered him up the stairs and the bemused young man barely had time to drain his cup before Holmes indicated that he should, once more, take up his father's letter.

Part Two

THE GIANT RAT OF SUMATRA

CHAPTER SIX

THE CULT OF THE RAT

Without questioning this sudden need for urgency Daniel Collier lit up the obligatory panatella and picked up his father's tale where he had left off. Holmes, in turn, lit a cigarette and stared intently at our young client, as if his eyes were boring into his head in an effort to extract the truth from within.

From there it was my intention to proceed to Singapore, via the Nicobar Islands and then to cross the treacherous straits of Malacca to the port of Medan and the capital city of northern Sumatra. By adopting this most complicated route I had hoped to avoid the political maelstrom that was Aceh.

At first it seemed that I was to fall at the first hurdle; after all, an isolated penal colony that was home to a few British troops, convicted criminals and a small number of fierce-looking indigenous pygmies was not exactly teeming with available transport for a bedraggled explorer!

However, the good fortune with which my journeys, so far, had been blessed, had not yet deserted me. Upon landing with the crew from the supply ship, I was led at once by a huge, brusque corporal to the office of his commanding officer. I could not, in all honesty, describe Lieutenant John Sterling as a friend, indeed the only previous occasion of our acquaintance had been the time when he had rescued me from a drunken brawl, in which I had become embroiled during the first of my visits to Bombay.

Nonetheless, he seemed to remember me well and could not have been more accommodating and co-operative. He was evidently glad of this opportunity to converse with someone who had not become sullied by this 'God-forsaken hole' and he even brought out a bottle of a surprisingly fine whisky, which he had secreted in the base of his desk drawer. Over this most welcome drink I briefly outlined to him the intention behind my proposed trip to Sumatra, and my motives seemed to galvanize his willingness to assist still further.

Sterling instructed the commander of the supply ship to divert his route back to Calcutta by way of Singapore. After all, the only cargo on the return trip was to have been the prisoners' letters home, and Sterling considered those to be of a low priority. He even detached two native subalterns[1] from his unit, to act both as my porters and my guides and one of these, a young giant of a man called Santi Patel, had a good knowledge of Sumatra from the time he had spent there as a youth.

My other companion was to be a quiet young man, Pritesh Chundrasama, who was a devout Hindu and sported quite the largest and densest beard that I had ever seen. I should imagine that any number of rare species had made their home amongst its luxuriant curls! However, this prodigious appendage would in no way hamper Pritesh's knowledge of Hindu temples, which would certainly prove to be invaluable.

Sterling found me a bunk for the only night that I was to spend on the Andamans and the following morning I had the unusual luxury of having my possessions and equipment loaded for me, back on to the small supply ship that was to ferry us across to Singapore. We anchored off of the Nicobar Islands for only as long as it took to collect the mail from this tiny outpost and a comfortable crossing soon found us amidst the bustle of the teeming, opulent metropolis that was Singapore.

I had not either the time or the means fully to enjoy the luxurious facilities that were so obviously available. I only had the use of Pritesh and Santi's services for a limited period and besides, it was my intention to track down the Ghadar and their valuable prize before they could have the chance to disappear completely amongst the dense forests with which Sumatra was so richly endowed.

So it was with a large proportion of my ever dwindling funds that I secured the use of a small, single-masted fishing boat on which I intended to complete the final stage of my Odyssey. It was a decision that very nearly cost us our lives!

The straits of Malacca, which separate Sumatra from the rest of Indonesia, were the only means of access available to me, given my aversion to the fierce conflict that was continually blighting my most obvious port of call, namely Aceh. The straits provided me with direct access to the port and regional capital of Medan, and their fierce currents guaranteed me a swift crossing.

However, as with the fastest of mustangs, the current's incredible speed came at a dangerous cost, for they are nigh on uncontrollable. My maritime ambition certainly exceeded the size of my craft and almost from the first, we were being vigorously tested by the fearsome tides that seemed to swirl around us from every point of the compass.

To begin with, while I manned the rudder Pritesh and Santi strained together in their efforts at controlling the sail. However, by the time that we were halfway across, our efforts were beginning to appear to be as futile as they were reckless. The infamous currents of the straits of Malacca evidently had not earned their reputation without good reason and before long the strong, erratic winds were pulling the mast and sail to their very limits.

87

Furthermore, I soon discovered that my rudder was all but useless and I eventually abandoned it in favour of taking some more effective measures.

I helped Pritesh and Santi to pull in the sail and lower the mast before we decided to lash them down, together with all of our possessions, underneath a large oilskin sheet that we had brought along for this purpose. With the entire deck now covered in the oilskin the three of us were now reduced to clinging on to the heavy ropes that secured it, and we each offered up suitable prayers to our respective gods!

It is, indeed, a most humbling experience to realize that your fate and life itself, have been taken from your hands and abilities and then entrusted to destiny and the harsh elements with which you have been bombarded. The salt from the waves stung our eyes and their chill came close to numbing our fingers, yet still we clung on to the life-preserving ropes.

Occasionally I lifted up my head and glanced towards my stalwart companions. I was thankful to see that they were enduring their suffering with a stoic calmness and bravery and were clinging on to the lashings with a most admirable tenacity. By the time that the elements had finally exhausted themselves, so, indeed, had we three, and we were all unconscious when we eventually reached the lush, green shoreline of Sumatra. The currents of the straits of Malacca had fulfilled their obligations and we were eventually aroused when our miraculous craft shuddered to a halt against a tree-lined sandbank.

As we struggled to our feet we looked about us, confused as to our exact location and yet smiling towards each other with relief that we were still alive. Before we began to explore our immediate surroundings, we decided to untie the ropes to determine how much, if any, of our supplies had survived the crossing. To our great joy it appeared that the oilskin had certainly done its job well and before long we gorged ourselves on chunks of bread and some surprisingly fresh mangoes. Amazingly my cigarettes and matches remained as dry as when I had first stowed them away and I gratefully put these into immediate employ!

With our strength now regained, we managed to haul the boat away from the sandbank and drag it into a more secluded area of coast from where we could decide in which direction we should strike out. In the absence of a point of reference, any examination of my maps proved to be futile. However, by using my compass I dispatched Santi to the north and Pritesh in a southerly direction in the hope that at least one of them would return with news of a useful starting point for our further travels.

If I had been hoping for a speedy response I was to be seriously disappointed, for it was to be a full three hours and several more cigarettes before a dejected Pritesh returned to our tiny camp, empty handed. He had maintained the course that I had prescribed for him, but all that he had encountered was a never ending forest that became thicker and more impassable with every stride that he took. Our hopes, therefore, rested upon Santi's broad shoulders and the north.

This time our wait was not a lengthy one and Santi was striding in the manner of a triumphant returning hero when he eventually came into view. As it turned out, he was not unjustified in doing so. He had just returned from a small isolated village that was perched upon the banks of a tributary to the important Alas river. Furthermore he had previously met some of the families who lived there, and two brothers were prepared to assist us in hauling our boat to the Alas tributary in order to repair and relaunch it.

The task we had set our ourselves was not without its difficulties, but with the help of Santi's friends we managed to fell enough small trees from which to fashion a rolling trolley upon which to transport the boat. Fortunately the terrain we were traversing was remarkably level and although the journey seemed to be considerably longer than the two miles that it actually was, we managed to complete it just before nightfall, with our boat and equipment intact.

Before turning in for the night I expressed my surprise at the stringent protective measures that were being taken around such a strategically insignificant outpost. Lines of menacing, sharply pointed fencing, interspersed by large open fires that were constantly being stoked, were set up along every inch of the village's small perimeter. In my view this appeared to be a disproportionate precaution for a village so far removed from the conflict in Aceh.

With some difficulty it was explained to me that during the past year two young children had been carried off by a rare man-eating tiger, indigenous to the shores of Sumatra. Understandably the villagers were determined that this tragedy should not be repeated. However, and despite these determined precautions, I endured a most fitful night's sleep and I maintained a loaded revolver by my side.

After two days of hard work the repairs to our boat had been completed and, as a final act of kindness, Santi's friends helped us achieve a successful launch. The tide was in our favour and soon we found ourselves drifting serenely downstream towards our original destination, namely the port of Medan. Upon our arrival we managed to secure the boat discreetly and while Pritesh and I endeavoured to replenish the supplies, Santi went off to enquire into the movements of the Ghadar.

As it happened Medan turned out to be a far larger and more cosmopolitan municipality than I had expected, and it soon became apparent to me that this newly found commercial affluence was due in part to the conflict in Aceh. Traders in gold and black pepper, Sumatra's most sought-after exports, were being forced to move their point of trade to a safer harbour, and I was by no means out of place amongst such a motley collection of international traders....

After a period of much hesitation in his reading, no doubt as a result of his father's deteriorating writing style, Collier suddenly broke off entirely. Inexplicably and for the first time since Collier had began to read, Holmes seemed to lose his concentration. He slapped his hand down hard on the arm of his chair, while letting out a high-pitched yelp. Then he jumped up and, after lighting a cigarette which he smoked feverishly, Holmes began to pace back and forth in front of the fire.

'In heaven's name, Holmes! I cannot, for the life of me imagine what has disturbed you so,' I exclaimed with some concern and confusion.

Holmes stopped his pacing and looked from Collier to me and back again. Somewhat taken aback by the attention that his exclamation had generated, Holmes smiled awkwardly and thought long and hard before replying to my anxious remark.

'Oh, it was nothing more alarming than an attack of leg cramp, I assure you.' He began to stretch his legs while he was speaking.

While it is true to say that Holmes was prone to sit with his legs tightly crossed beneath him when in a state of deep concentration, a position from which it is possible to contract one's calf muscles, I had never known him to be so afflicted before. I could not imagine another reason for his strange reaction, but did not dare to question him further in the presence of our client.

'Mr Collier, I apologize for my abrupt behaviour, but I sense that there was a reason for your prolonged hesitation,' Holmes explained.'

'Though it was a surprising juncture for him to do so, my father decided to conclude his second letter at this point. As you have no doubt observed for yourself, it is becoming increasingly difficult for me to make sense of the remainder and I was merely steeling myself before continuing.'

Holmes nodded his acceptance of Collier's statement.

'His actions are not hard to understand when you consider that from this point onwards he was not certain as to when he would next have an opportunity to dispatch another letter to you. After all, he was about to embark upon a journey into uncharted waters. His time in Medan was the ideal moment for him to send this,' Holmes concluded.

'Now I understand,' I stated quietly, although in reality my remark could not have been further from the truth. I was not convinced by Holmes's claim to have been attacked by leg cramp and I searched for another reason in the last few lines of Collier's letter. Interesting though the narrative undoubtedly was, I could find nothing in his references to gold and pepper-traders, or Santi's enquiries into the movements of the Ghadar, that would normally have provoked such a strident reaction from Holmes.

'Can you confirm that the postmark upon your father's second letter was from Medan?' Holmes asked suddenly, so breaking up my chain of thought.

'I presume that he had entrusted the letter to either Pritesh or Santi to post on their way back to the Andaman Islands, for the envelope bore the mark of Singapore,' Collier replied.

'That seems to imply that he did not expect to be returning by that route himself,' I observed.

Holmes turned suddenly towards me, staring intently as if my words had instigated a further chain of thought within him.

'Very likely not, although, of course, it would be a grave error for us to jump to any conclusions before we hear the remainder of Sir Michael Collier's journals. However, the conclusion of the second letter presents me with the perfect opportunity to stretch my troubled legs and also for you, Mr Collier, to rest your aching eyes.' Holmes still appeared to have been gravely distracted and he added quietly, in fact almost to himself: 'Of course there is still the problem of the third letter. I shall be out for an hour or so and I suggest that you make good use of my room.' Holmes made this seem more of a directive than a suggestion and one that Collier had begun to act upon even before Holmes had left the room.

So I was to be left to my own devices. Remaining heedful of Holmes's earlier and most alarming warning, I resolved not to allow our young client out of my sight for even the briefest moment. I turned my chair around so that it then faced the door to Holmes's room and I took down my copy of *Journeys Through the Lands of the Bible* by Sir Michael Collier.

I decided that to speculate as to which direction Holmes's thoughts had now taken him would prove to be a pointless exercise. Far better, I reasoned, to reacquaint myself with Sir Michael's earlier writings, and perhaps I might learn something by comparing the style and contents with those of the letters.

Unfortunately my mind was by now saturated with the travels and tribulations of the great explorer and, despite my greatest efforts at preventing it happening, within a few moments I had drifted off into a subconscious world of caped phantoms and Eastern holy men.

I was only aroused from my slumber when Collier's praiseworthy tome slipped from my loosened grasp and thumped to the floor at my feet. I was in a state of blind panic when I glanced at the clock and realized that a full two hours had elapsed since Holmes's abrupt departure. Upon opening the door to his room, which I did with great care, I was much relieved to find Daniel Collier spread out upon the bed cover, fully clothed and clearly in a state of great exhaustion.

The potential consequences of his having slipped passed me while I had been asleep were too dire even to contemplate and my hand was shaking as I lit my cigarette. I moved over to the window as the ever darkening twilight was gradually seeping beneath the edges of our blinds. All the while I was wondering at Holmes's whereabouts and why he did not come home.

When Holmes did at last return I soon realized that I had no need to enquire as to the success of his mission; I merely had to observe. He was barely able to suppress a smile of intense satisfaction and the sparks of triumph flashed from his eyes as they darted from me to Collier and back to me once more.

'I apologize for my protracted absence, gentlemen, but I can assure you that it was absolutely necessary. Oh, Watson, our journey surely now begins! However, you should both be glad to know that I have arranged with Mrs Hudson for our evening meal, after which, Mr Collier, I would prevail upon you to conclude your father's most remarkable tale.'

'I should be glad to,' Collier replied. 'Although I should point out that the conclusion is somewhat more disjointed than that which has gone before. Indeed, the third and last letter does not even take up the tale from the moment that the second breaks off.' He explained this almost apologetically.

Holmes dismissed this with a wave of his hand. 'I assume that the final letter bore the postmark from Aceh?' he asked.

'It did! However did you know?' Collier asked incredulously.

'Ah, so I can see now that my little excursion was not entirely fruitless.' Holmes laughed.

At this juncture a timely knock on the door announced the arrival of our food and a moment later we were all tucking into a most succulent rack of lamb. Once the meal had been concluded and we had enjoyed a satisfying smoke and a glass of port, Daniel Collier unfolded his crumpled package for the last time.

I should emphasize here that at this stage of his narrative, no doubt due to the gradual deterioration in both his circumstances and his physical condition, Sir Michael Collier's writing was becoming increasingly patchy and erratic. In spite of these impediments his son toiled away gamely enough; however, Holmes

seemed impatient with his efforts and I sensed that he was gradually becoming somewhat frustrated. This was undoubtedly due
to fact that the next phase of his investigations was now uppermost in his thoughts.

For the sake of my readers I have endeavoured to smooth over
Daniel Collier's hesitant, stuttering reading style and to link
together these passages as coherently as possible.

It was with a heavy heart that I finally released Pritesh and Santi
from their obligations to me. I insisted that they should return,
by way of Singapore, to my benefactor on the Andaman Islands,
Lieutenant John Sterling. Even at the last, both Pritesh and Santi
proved to be as good as their word. Santi's investigations on my
behalf had revealed that a band of Indian liberationists were
rumoured to have taken refuge amongst the ruined remains of
a large Hindu temple that was to be found upon the banks of
Lake Toba.

For his part Pritesh helped me garner whatever meagre
supplies that my depleted funds would allow, although I ensured
that these would run to a healthy supply of ammunition for my
revolver. As I packed my bags aboard the boat, I was reassured by
the sight of these rounds, for the tales of man-eating tigers and
small isolated tribes that still practised forms of cannibalism,
convinced me that before my journey's end they could prove to
be more valuable to me than any food and drink.

Finally, Pritesh informed me that the temple that I was
seeking was undoubtedly the famed temple called Portibi or, as
it was known from its Bartak translation, In This World. It was
thought to have been built by workers from the Hindu kingdom
of Panai in approximately 10 AD, and its style certainly hailed
from southern India.

I shook his shoulders violently in the excitement of my realization that the circle of my voyage of discovery was all but

complete. Of course there would still be much danger and many hazards to endure before I would be able to reach my goal, but something told me that the temple of Portibi would prove to be the culmination of my journey.

After supplying me with a rough map and much heartfelt advice, Pritesh and Santi departed for the quay of Begawan harbour. As I watched them walk reluctantly away from me I realized that, for the first time since I had set off from Nirvana so many months ago, I was now to be totally alone.

This feeling of isolation was no more noticeable than when I eventually clambered aboard my sorry boat and stowed away my gear. My heart was full of trepidation, for I had no knowledge of what truly lay ahead, nor had I yet formulated a plan as to my course of action should I be successful in my search for the temple of Portibi, the supposed refuge of the Ghadar movement.

Perhaps no plan existed in my head because, in my heart of hearts, I did not really expect ever to reach Portibi, let alone retrieve the fabled beladau, my means of saving an empire! Should I fail in my attempt then surely this would indeed be my final journey and conceivably my quest would culminate in the way that I had always intended. Not withstanding these dark and portentous thoughts, I did push off from the bank and began rowing slowly upstream along one of a myriad of tiny tributaries that fed the Deli River delta.

Perusing Pritesh's map, I realized that if I maintained my compass at a point of north by northwest, each tributary would lead me into another and then another until I should eventually cascade into Lake Toba through the series of waterfalls that were fed by the waters of the Barisan mountains and the Alas river.

As I moved slowly along my course I was left constantly amazed by the complexity and rich diversity of the terrain that I was travelling through. Mercifully the climate in northern Sumatra proved to be surprisingly temperate, so therefore the

lush and impenetrable forests did not have the humid, debilitating effect of so many that I had encountered in other parts of
the world. Indeed, as I passed through one of the many limestone
gorges that ripped a tear through this carpet of green the
temperature became uncomfortably chilly, to the extent that it
left me longing for a swift return to the cover that the forest
afforded me.

That is not to say that my labours at the oar were rendered any
less arduous by the absence of humidity and before too long it
became obvious to me that the forty or so miles that made the
distance from Medan to Lake Toba, would seem considerably
longer than that by the time that I had completed them.
Furthermore, the lake itself was fully fifty miles in length and I
had no means of knowing how many of those miles I would have
to cover before I came upon the temple of Portibi somewhere
along its shores.

By the time that I decided to stop for the night I estimated that
I had covered no more than four or five miles. I soon realized
that at my current rate of progress, both my strength and
supplies would be exhausted long before I had completed my
journey. It was a sobering thought and one that made me grateful
for the full bottle of whisky that was nestling safely underneath
the rest of my supplies.

Before I tied up my boat for the night, I ensured that there was
a comfortable distance between myself and any of the numerous
tiny Bartak villages that seemed to pepper the course of the
river. I hurriedly assembled a small shelter from a collection of
light timber and tarpaulin that I had brought along for that
purpose and before long a small fire was illuminating my humble
campsite.

Once I had consumed a light supper of corned beef and bread
it occurred to me that the lack of company would not be the only
disadvantage to my being alone. The jungle in which I was

encamped was positively teeming with a variety of potentially hostile wild life. It was, therefore, imperative that the size and intensity of my fire was maintained throughout the night, to ward off any threats. Yet who was there to stoke it while I took a few hours sleep? Who was there to keep my revolver cocked and ready to fire at a moment's notice? The answer to both of these questions was the same. Each night I was destined to maintain a long and sleepless vigil.

My slow progress was also causing me some concern. I decided to abandon one of my oars the following morning and to continue my journey by paddling with only one, in a canoe-like fashion. These continuing thoughts, a substantial swig from my bottle of whisky and the glow from my essential fire eventually lulled me into an most reluctant and dangerous slumber.

I awoke with a start and a severe crick in my neck, as I had slept in an upright position, and I realized how perilous my lack of consciousness might well have proved to be. I looked about me as the earliest traces of dawn were encroaching upon the domain of the dark and treacherous night. I decided that the centre of the stream might prove to be the safest place for me to obtain some rest.

I fashioned an anchor from a piece of cord and a medium-sized boulder, then let it drop once I was certain that my boat was equidistant from the river's banks. There I was to sleep until the noon sun awoke me with its intense glare, which was only relieved by the shadows of the overhanging trees. Now fully refreshed I immediately put my paddling theory into practice and soon realized that it was to be borne out. Assisted by a bubbling downstream current, I doubled my rate of progress of the previous day and continued my journey with a renewed optimism.

As I progressed further, the width of the stream appeared to be gradually lessening. This surprised me somewhat, as I had actually been expecting the stream to broaden as I drew closer to Lake Toba. Was I on the intended tributary? Was I even moving in the right direction? I could not be sure. My only certainty was that the thickening jungle was gradually closing in upon the diminishing water, way in front of me. It was as if I was being sucked inexorably into the very womb of Mother Nature herself!

That evening, as I lay on the bottom of my little boat, exhausted by my day's efforts, it occurred to me that there was a lesson for all of us to be learned from the vast, primeval forest that now surrounded me. When viewed individually the lotus flower is undoubtedly a creation of extraordinary beauty, whereas the humble weed or nettle is surely something to be avoided and shunned. However, when seen as tiny components of this vast green tapestry, neither the lotus flower nor the weed are distinguishable from the whole and each appears to be as beautiful as the other.

I could not help but wonder how much hatred could have been avoided and how many lives would have been saved had mankind ever seen itself in this manner. Sadly, there are too many of us who see themselves as lotus flowers and therefore perceive everyone else as nettles. That is mankind's greatest folly and the cause of all of its miseries.

'Mr Collier!' Holmes exclaimed suddenly. 'Your father is undoubtedly a wise man and a great visionary!'

Clearly moved by Holmes's compliments and what he knew was about to follow, Daniel Collier put down his father's parchment once again. He began to pace back and forth, in front of the fireplace while smoking what proved to be the last of his hitherto seemingly inexhaustible supply of panatellas. Holmes eyed him quizzically and with some concern.

'Mr Collier, the hour grows late. Would you prefer to continue in the cold light of day?' Holmes offered.

Collier appeared to be alarmed at this suggestion, perhaps not wishing to impose himself upon us further.

'With your indulgence, gentlemen, I should really prefer to conclude the matter at this sitting,' Collier quietly requested. Holmes agreed with a solemn nod of his head.

'By all means!' I concurred, while ignoring my own misgivings regarding the lateness of the hour.

Collier resumed his seat and gratefully continued reading.

My dear boy, please forgive the deterioration in both my writing style and coherency. As you might well imagine, my present conditions are far from conducive to good writing and I am certain that by now you are finding the task of deciphering my ramblings somewhat trying. If, indeed, you are still reading them at all!

In the hope that you are, I have decided to précis each of my day's events and experiences and set them out in the form of a diary. My surroundings seem to remain unchanged for days on end and as I have no scientific means of calculating the distances that I am covering, it is becoming increasingly difficult for me to distinguish one day from the next. My proposed diary format will help me maintain some cohesion and chronology to my life and to monitor the passing of time since the day of my departure from Medan. I am certain that no more than forty-eight hours have passed since I bade farewell to Pritesh and Santi and as I put my pen down, for the night, I now look forward to my third day upon the river.

Day Three

My improved progress of yesterday has slowed considerably today as I battle against a current bound for Medan. I suppose that my reduced stroke rate may also be due to my dwindling supplies that are now barely sufficient to bind body and soul together. I have resorted to plunging a sharpened shaft of wood into the river in the hope that I might extract an edible fish. Worryingly, the fast-running, shallow waters have produced nothing larger than the size of my hand and my only sustenance is provided by the nuts and fruit from the overhanging trees.

As a last recourse I have thrown my fears and caution to the wind and decided to land at the very next Bartak village that I come to. Whatever my fate might be at their hands, it cannot be worse than the slow withering decline and death that can be the only conclusion to my continuing to remain drifting in midstream.

Day Four

What a revelation the charming people of the village have proved to be. The majority of its inhabitants spoke a smattering of English, as a result of their brief contact with European missionaries in the early nineties, before the fighting in Aceh intensified. Despite their forbidding appearance and reputation, I discovered that the people of the Bartak were both friendly and courteous and practised nothing more ferocious than the writing of romantic and sentimental songs, the rendering of which they frequently treated me to during my extended stay there.

Their chief allowed me to share his hut with his entire family and graciously allowed me a share of every provision that came their way. The next day they invited me to accompany them upon one of their all-important hunting trips and they promised me a feast of succulent boar meat the following evening.

Day Five

The villagers were as good as their word and, at break of dawn on the following morning, all the able-bodied men set off together, brandishing their hunting sticks. As we drew closer to our quarry these were rattled loudly together as a means of harrying the boars into the direction of the 'throwers'. The march was long and arduous, through the densest part of the forest, yet it afforded me the opportunity to observe a family of the elusive orang-utan apes who ignored us as we marched past them.

It was astonishing to see how much of their behaviour and how many of their mannerisms are shared with their human cousins and neighbours. It is hardly surprising, therefore, that the Bartak name for them translates to 'The Man of the Forest'. I also had my first view, though thankfully from some distance, of the feared and unique Sumatran tiger. It was clearly stalking us from a grassy ridge and as soon as it came into view, the Bartak began to beat their sticks together ferociously. Once I had realized that this was not having the desired effect, I fired off two overhead shots from my revolver. The tiger immediately disappeared and I had further ingratiated myself with my hosts, who were most impressed by my 'weapon of thunder'.

Day Six

When we eventually returned to the village the following evening, it was as conquering heroes, with our bag of two magnificent beasts as evidence of our total triumph. The women immediately set to work on building a large roaring fire and preparing the vegetables, while we set the boars up on spits and prepared large jugs of a most potent and pungent brew, fermented from a strange-looking orange root vegetable that grew throughout the jungle in great abundance.

Day Seven

My hosts knew that it was my intention to take my leave of them on the following morning and they were, evidently, as reluctant to see me go as I was to resume my journey. Nevertheless, by the time that I had managed to rouse myself from my stupor, I discovered that my boat had been loaded with as much roasted boar meat and fresh fruit as it could possibly hold.

With renewed strength I pushed my boat hard that day and I was able to continue with my efforts until well after twilight. By the time that I had dropped my makeshift anchor for the night, every nocturnal beast of the jungle was in full chorus and yet, as I was quietly chewing on my meat, I felt sure that I could hear the sound of an immense body of moving water somewhere further down the stream. After I had completed my meal, I drained the last drop from my whisky bottle and, as I watched it bobbing its way gently back towards Medan, I wondered with excitement what lay ahead of me round the next bend of the river.

Day Eight

The expectations that I had been harbouring throughout the long night soon evaporated once I realized that the sound of rushing water had undoubtedly been nothing more than a creation inside my sore, intoxicated head. As I moved further inland there was certainly no doubt that the river was gradually widening and quickening. However, the large body of water that I had envisaged drawing me into the magnificence of Lake Toba still would not reveal itself to me.

The number of bends that I had rounded that day had been countless and each time that the river had straightened I had expected to find the water falling away directly in front of me. It was dark again before at last I gave up all hope of success for that day and I flung down my oar in frustration as I despaired of ever reaching the accursed lake! My temper was not lightened when I realized that the cigarette that I had enjoyed after my supper was to be my last. I strained my ears for even a trace of the sound that I had thought that I had heard the night before, but again I was to be disappointed. When at last I did fall asleep it was in a state of great anxiety.

Day Nine

I began the day by consuming the last of the fruit that the Bartak had kindly given to me, although I must confess that I set off that morning with very little enthusiasm. My progress was slow once more and as the river continued to widen I realized that I was losing the blessed shelter from the afternoon sun that the over-hanging trees had formerly provided me with. On this stretch of the river the water was now clear and fresh so that thirst was no longer a problem. However this endless meandering was causing me to question the validity of my reasons for being here and, indeed, my very motives for desiring the recovery of the beladau.

Potentially this ancient and sacred weapon could be used as a means to incite rebellion. Yet who was I to condemn the cause of political freedom. A patriotic Englishman? Certainly. The saviour of an empire that stood upon the remains of a proud and ancient civilization?

I was left to ponder upon that principle, which was of my own creation. Who was I to say that the existence of the lotus flower was any more deserving than that of the thorn? Indeed, who was the lotus flower and who was the thorn? Which was the occupier and which the occupied? These questions were constantly hammering away inside my burning head.

At the conclusion of another fruitless day of toil, I decided to set up my small camp once more, upon the bank of the river. No longer being fearful of the Bartak, it seemed to me that the advantages far outweighed the disadvantages. Delicious fresh fruit was plentifully available and I had become indifferent to the threat posed by the elusive renegade tiger. Admittedly, I still established my precautionary fire, but on this occasion I did not worry unduly about maintaining it throughout the night.

Ultimately it was my own thoughts, constantly nagging at me and harassing me, that prevented me from sleeping that night and not the threatening roar that echoed in the distance.

Day Ten

I suppose that I must have finally succumbed to exhaustion some time just before dawn, because the next thing that I was aware of was the glare of the climbing sun striking down upon my sore and heavy eyes. Before long I was to realize that the glare was about to be obliterated.

I was at once alerted to an unnatural and all embracing silence that seemed to have affected every living creature within the forest. Their instincts were heedful of an imminent natural disturbance and one glance towards the north confirmed to me the source of their fear. An enormous bank of dark and ominous clouds had been seated above the Barisan mountains for the past few days. They had been motionless, as though they were attached to the very peaks themselves, and they had posed no immediate threat.

However, as I looked towards them now, I could see that they had shifted dramatically and that they were virtually overhead!

The first rolls of thunder were enough to convince me that now was the time to break up my camp with all speed. I placed my belongings in the base of my boat underneath the tarpaulin and a further covering of oilskin. Once I was certain that my papers and equipment were secure and strapped down, I made good my moorings and then crawled in after them. There, with God's grace, to ride out the storm.

Day Eleven

The tempest continued, unabated, for many hours and as it turned out, well into the night. Never before had I felt as if my own destiny was out of my hands and would be determined by a higher force. As I lay there for an interminable length of time, I could feel my craft being continually buffeted by the maelstrom that the river had now become. Time and again I was convinced that my moorings had been wrenched free and that I was to be sent hurtling into oblivion. Yet somehow they held fast. The sound of the rain as it crashed down upon my shelter was deafening and I felt as if I was being attacked by a thousand hammers!

Then it was over, as I always knew it would be, and I made my first few tentative advances from beneath my shelter. Miraculously my craft and I had escaped intact, although the transformation that had taken place amongst my surroundings was dramatic. The level of the river had risen by several inches and it was running now rather than meandering as before. I was not alone either. The creatures that had hitherto remained hidden in a stunned silence, now rediscovered their voices. The chattering of the monkeys, the shrill calls of a thousand tropical birds all blended into a cacophony of expressed joy.

A small herd of deer joined me at the water's edge and further downstream I could see a family of elephants enjoy a bath in the cooling and fast-running stream. Then I heard it! The sound that had been haunting me for the past few days. It was rising above that wondrous symphony and sounding much closer that it had done two nights before. The roar of water crashing down in force into an unfathomable abyss.

I could only assume that the course of the river was so tortuous and its bends so extreme that when I had first heard the sound of the falls they were then lying parallel to my own location. This time there was no mistaking their sound nor their close proximity. The falls of Sipiso-Piso at Tonggino and potentially my gateway to Lake Toba were, undoubtedly, just a few bends of the river away from me!

I collected a handful of the foul-smelling, but beautiful tasting, durian fruit, which seemed to be in such plentiful supply, and decided to take advantage of the fast-running waters by setting off immediately towards the falls. My papers were still safe and secure from the night before and I was as prepared as I possibly could be for my descent into the unknown.

The bends of the river shunted and diverted me this way and that; however the roar of those majestic falls remained undiminished. The river widened noticeably as I cut my way through one final limestone gorge, and as I emerged back into the sunlight I realized that barely one hundred yards ahead, the river suddenly seemed to vanish!

I subsequently discovered that the falls were three hundred and sixty feet deep and yet the mist from the crashing waters below surged back upwards and towards me with a howl. The speed of the water was such that my oar was now rendered useless and I would not have been able to stop myself had I wanted to. I stowed away my oar, leant back as far as I could and clung on as hard as I could to the strapping. Not for the first time my life was in the hands of another, and with a rush I tipped over the edge.

The spray clouded my vision of the foot of the falls and the descent was steeper than I had imagined it to be. For a few moments my life hung in the balance as I veered downwards. However, with immense relief I found that my boat remained as straight as an arrow and ploughed smoothly into the deep pool below. Upon making impact with the water I was unable to avoid a jagged rocky outcrop that protruded from the depths and its edge caught the side of my head, close to the temple. I was still conscious when the boat temporarily submerged, then righted itself again and then ...

Oblivion!

Day ?

I could not tell for how long I had been lying in the bottom of my boat in a state of unconsciousness. It might have been for a few hours, or it might have been days. Upon awakening I discovered that my new surroundings were so surreal compared with those that my hazy memory could recall that I was not certain whether I had entered the gates of paradise itself, if that was indeed to be my final port of call.

If it is, well then the island of Samosir, positioned in the centre of Lake Toba, would be its perfect setting. As a point of interest, Samosir is all that remains of the summit of a gigantic, volcanic mountain that erupted millions of years ago. Its destructive power was of such magnitude as to produce the vast lake upon which I was now floating.

Apparently my boat had drifted away from the base of the falls, while I had been in my coma, and I was now only a few hundred yards away from Samosir itself. It is reassuring to think that so much beauty can be created from an occurrence of such horrific destruction. The circumference of the island was fringed by a line of fine white sand. In its centre a clutch of tall elegant trees proudly looked over wave upon wave of lush green forests and tiny, sparkling waterfalls. Here and there I could detect a small clearing or two, containing a collection of buildings that were clearly Bartak in construction.

I decided to make for the nearest of these, set but a few hundred yards from the beach. I had heard that the Toba Bartak were somewhat fiercer in their appearance and behaviour than their cousins further downstream. I discovered that the first half of the statement was true, but not the second. I had hoped that the inhabitants of the village of Parapat would provide me with a place to rest and recuperate for a few days. But, more important, that they might save me a considerable amount of time and effort by pinpointing the Temple of Portibi.

I was delighted when these people proved to be every bit as kind-hearted and hospitable as I had hoped, but distressed and horrified when they informed me that the temple that I sought was not to be found on the shores of Lake Toba at all, but in a place called the 'Holy Forest' on the Alas river!

Could Pritesh have been so seriously misinformed? Had somebody deliberately misled him in an attempt to cover the movements of the Ghadar?

I could not contemplate prolonging my journey even further, nor did I possess the resources to consider undertaking it. In fact I was on the point of despair when a young woman, Rashini, who had tended to my wounds upon my arrival, provided me with a third choice.

Was it not possible that a temple such as described by Pritesh did exist somewhere along the shores of the lake and that it was merely its name of which he had been misinformed? Of course it was possible! I was so delighted at this suggestion that before I realized what I was doing I had kissed and embraced the beautiful Rashini. She was not averse to such intimacy and it felt natural that she should return my embrace. It was all I could do to persuade her to lead me to a village elder who knew of a likely site for the temple that I sought. Reluctantly she did so, but I knew then that it would difficult for me to take my leave of her the following morning.

The elder knew of a large complex of temples further along the eastern coast line, that had sadly fallen into a state of ruin and decay. I was amazed to hear that he believed it had been built over 1,000 years ago by the same Panai builders that had constructed the temple of Portibi. Furthermore, it had been dedicated to Shiva and inscribed with his name and symbols, the very same god that Bal Gangadhar Tilak had invoked when he had first rallied the Ghadar extremists!

By the time he had further informed me that one of the temple courtyards was adorned with a beautiful bronze female statue that had been brought to these lands from southern India, I knew that when I awoke on the following morning, I would be embarking upon the final stage of my long journey. I was pleased to note that the Toba Bartak fermented the same potent orange brew that I had previously enjoyed.

I celebrated the wonderful news with a healthy cup or two of this strange drink and when I awoke the next day I prayed forgiveness from your mother as I realized that Rashini was still lying next to me!

Day ?

The entire village turned out to watch me row across to the mainland coast of the lake. Although the tearful Rashini refused to join them, I would not be diverted from the task that lay ahead of me.

That same elder had also warned me to be on my guard. Apparently occasional groups of marauding Dutch troops made use of the temple ruins as a temporary camp while rounding up refugees fleeing from Aceh. Although German missionaries were the only white people whom the Toba Bartak had encountered for many months, the elder still felt that it would best for me to remain vigilant. He then made an obscure and tentative reference to a group of vigilantes known as the 'Cult of the Giant Rat'. However, he would not be drawn further when I questioned him as to its nature.

Acting upon his advice, I ensured that my revolver was dry and fully loaded, and as I drew closer to the supposed site of the temple I maintained a smooth and silent stroke of the oar. Unfortunately the lush green forest extended all the way down to the actual water's edge and I realized that this would prohibit me from gaining a view of the temple in advance of my approach. I thought it best to remain still and silent for a moment or two in case there were any sounds ahead that might aid me in my search.

Fresh tobacco leaves grew in abundance in the surrounding

hills and I had fashioned for myself a number of moist green cigars before I had left the village. I lit up one of these, at this opportune moment and sat there smoking in silence, until the waves of heady nausea that my cigar had induced caused me to hurl the remainder into the water. I decided to allow the others enough time to dry out, before indulging in them again.

I looked back towards the village, which had by now disappeared into the distance, and with a resigned shrug I continued upon my slow, painstaking progress. I had just rounded a shallow bend and crossed a small bay when I became aware of a fine plume of grey smoke rising above the tree-line that lay just ahead of me!

The implication of this was obvious. Unless I had been unfortunate enough to have stumbled across a troop of Dutch soldiers, I was now no more than a stone's throw away from the headquarters of the Ghadar movement. I hauled my boat on to the shore and tethered it securely before camouflaging it beneath some heavy foliage.

I was determined to ensure that my only means of making an urgent escape was safe and available to me at a moment's notice. Once I was satisfied that all was secure and with my last few belongings gathered into a tiny sack, I set off on foot towards the line of smoke.

CHAPTER SEVEN

A MASTER OF SILAT

As I drew ever closer to the object of my quest I strained both my eyes and ears for any confirmation that my search was drawing nearer to its conclusion. After I had been walking for barely fifty yards or so that confirmation became very much in evidence.

To begin with, I was sure that I could just make out the faint murmuring of voices coming from within a clearing just ahead of me. My blood chilled once I was certain that they were speaking in Gujarat, the dominant language of western India. Then, as I approached the clearing the decaying forms of red-clay pillars and intricately constructed domes loomed from behind the ever thinning line of trees, which had previously obscured them from me.

I dropped to the ground then and wriggled forward by using my knees and elbows, while the voices became ever louder and more distinct. The ancient edifices reared up all around me and I was left awestruck as I imagined how inspiring they must have looked all those centuries ago.

I lay there for several moments, lost within this world of a distant past. I had failed to notice the change in the direction from which the voices were now coming and was oblivious to the sounds of footsteps working their way around and behind me. Two straw sandals appeared in the corner of my eye. Two large shadows now loomed over me. Too late I realized the immediate danger that now confronted me. The futility of my resistance did not prevent me from trying to throw off two vicelike grips, which were clamped painfully on my shoulders.

I raised my hands above my head; then the butt of a rifle came crashing down upon it!

Days? Weeks?

A large bucket of icy water was sent crashing into my face. My attempts at wiping the water clear from my eyes were hampered by two bonds of rough cord that were biting deep into the skin around my wrists. The painful abrasions began to bleed as soon as I struggled to free myself, but my efforts were met by the sounds of coarse and mocking laughter.

I didn't know how long I had been unconscious. My eyes were sore and I was aware of dried blood down the side of my nose. The sun blazed angrily down, the glare increasing the terrible pain in my head. I growled a few choice expletives in the direction of my captives and my reward was a blow from another heavy object upon my skull. The last thing I remember, before losing consciousness once more, was two brutal sandals striking the side of my thighs as the laughter slowly drifted into the distance.

Night?

Two large logs, which had suddenly snapped and then collapsed into the centre of the dying fire, roused me from another night's sleep spent in captivity. I could not be sure of the time but the grey hue of the heavy sky indicated that it was still an hour or two before dawn. The sound from the fire had not, apparently, disturbed anybody else and since my bonds appeared to be unbreakable, I used these moments of silent solitude to acquaint myself with my surroundings.

A large makeshift camp had been erected within the court-yard of the decaying, complex of Hindu temples. The canvas, which had probably originated from British army issue, had been cleverly camouflaged with painted shades of greens and reds and the temple buildings themselves had been integrated into the camp wherever they had been sufficiently well-preserved to provide adequate shelter. Sadly, there were very few enough examples of these.

I was restricted from any further scrutiny of my surroundings by the impediment of my bonds and by the fact that the camp was, at last, beginning to stir. I recognized my two principle tormentors at once. They were both tall young men who sported untidy black beards and long dark kaftans. One of them, the stockier of the two, evidently felt some sympathy for my plight and he flung a large, pungent durian fruit into my lap as he passed by on his way to the lakeside for his morning bathe. This I ravenously devoured.

As a further group of men followed those two down to the waters, I could see that they were all similarly attired, and their loud, good natured camaraderie was evidence of a closely bonded brotherhood. They each carried a breech-loading rifle and ammunition belts were draped over their shoulders. I was left wondering for whom or what they were maintaining such high vigilance, and how much longer I was going to have to wait before I was to learn of my fate.

Once they returned to camp I was able to make out odd snatches of their conversation as they took breakfast around the rekindled fire. I understood that I was considered to be either a British or Dutch spy and that their leader, Tilat, otherwise known as the Giant Rat, would know what to do with me upon his return from his training in the mountains. As to the nature and purpose of this training, I could make nothing out. However, they speculated that my fate was not destined to be a pleasant one and they glared menacingly towards me as they let out yet another round of raucous laughter.

Any attempts that I made in striking up a stilted conversation were, at first, met with a stony silence. However, once I had managed to convince them of the dire necessity of my paying a visit to the lakeside myself, two guards temporarily released and escorted me, still brandishing their rifles, so that I could attend to my toilet. Although neither of them would divulge his name to me, nor the reason for their being encamped within the temple, I was able to glean some information from them on the way back to camp.

Although they were reticent in explaining their motives, they were more than happy to expand upon the subject of their revered leader. The man in whose hands my future wellbeing now rested was known as the 'Giant Rat' because of his extraordinary height and his ability in the monkey stance of the Indonesian martial art known as silat. I was familiar with this art as a result of my time spent in the Himalayas, the place of origin of nearly all of the styles of martial combat. However, the monkey form, also known as *dangyat monyet,* was a unique derivation that was based upon the movements of the poisonous Sumatran 'Rat Monkey'.

It was all I could do to suppress my excitement when I learnt that the form's principal weapons were a deadly strike of the palm and a razor-sharp curved blade known as a beladau! The 'Giant Rat' was an undoubted master in the use of both of these and he would soon return having spent several weeks in the mountains, in deep meditation and after further honing his unmatchable skills.

I felt it prudent, on my part, not to mention the fact that I already knew that I was in the hands of the Ghadah movement. Yet somehow, as I sat there for days on end listening to them talk, I began to realize that their aims were not those of a group set merely on a mindless quest for power. They wanted real political freedom for their people and would return to India to take it, once their associates were fully prepared.

Day ?

My guards began to sense that I could understand much of their conversations and that I was becoming a sympathetic listener. Furthermore, I was able to convince them that I was no military spy, but an explorer in search of the secrets and mysteries of ancient Hindu history. In fact I was so successful in this respect that the next time I was led down to the lake, on our return I was shown through to another courtyard wherein was enshrined the legendary golden statue of a beautiful female goddess that had been transported from Southern India centuries before. I was in little doubt that she was a depiction of Laksmi, the goddess of fortune and the third deity to whom the temple had been dedicated.

I was further pleased to note that, when I was eventually returned to my position by the fire, my bonds were now to be left unsecured, although my guards maintained their armed vigilance. I was now looking forward to the return of the 'Giant Rat' and not viewing it with my previous dread. I would not have to wait much longer.

Day ?

The return of Tilat could not have occurred under more dramatic circumstances. That evening another storm cloud had descended from the Barisans[1] and by the time that Tilat had entered the camp we were being bombarded by all the powers of a fully fledged tempest. My custodians ushered me into their shelter from where we watched the deluge wash away much of the camp. As soon as the storm was directly overhead, every flash of lightning was met by a deafening crack of thunder that seemed to make the very ground beneath us quake. A thousand artillery units would have been drowned out by this assault from the heavens. Then, in its very centre, an awe-inspiring vision suddenly appeared.

This manifestation was framed by shafts of violent white light, which surrounded him. He made no movements towards us, nor we to him, for he just stood there, fully upright and unaffected by the elements, as if he controlled them.

The 'Giant Rat' was certainly a giant, for he stood at well over six feet five inches, the hood and crimson robe that he wore making him appear to be all the taller and more awe-inspiring. He glided slowly past us, glancing neither to the left nor to the right, as he made his way towards an inner sanctum that seemed to be reserved for his use alone.

Since I was now in such close proximity to my captors it was easier for me to detect that they now regarded me with considerably less hostility and mistrust than they had at any time since my unfortunate, initial arrival at their camp. As I began to settle down for a cramped and uncomfortable night with them, I could only hope that their leader treated me with the same generous disposition as they had done.

I could barely contain my excitement at the very mention of this description of the 'Giant Rat' and, in anticipation of an untimely and unfortunate reaction from me, Holmes suddenly sprang up from his seat and put me off with a warning glare. Collier broke off from his reading and regarded Holmes with some surprise.

'I can assure you that we are rapidly approaching the final pages of what might possibly be the last words that I shall ever receive from my father,' Collier commented sadly and apologetically.

Holmes waved the apology aside.

'Before you conclude I am certain that Dr Watson has a specific question that he cannot wait to ask of you,' Holmes suggested mischievously, obviously after having changed his mind about maintaining discretion in front of Daniel Collier.

I was so taken aback by the nature of Holmes's surprising

suggestion that for a moment or two I was unable to formulate a coherent sentence. I slowly filled and then lit up a pipe.

'Please forgive me for the bizarre nature of my enquiry; however it might well prove to be of the utmost importance. Since your arrival in London have you been aware of anybody keeping you under surveillance and, more specifically, anyone vaguely resembling your father's description of the "Giant Rat of Sumatra"?' I eventually asked, somewhat clumsily.

Collier did not hesitate, even for an instant, before making his reply.

'I can state with the utmost certainty that I have not.' Then, having noted the looks of disappointment on both our faces, he added, 'However, that is hardly surprising when you consider that apart from a very short detour I came directly to your rooms from the station.'

'I did not notice any belongings of yours in the hallway below and I am certain that you did not travel all the way up from Cornwall bearing only the clothes upon your back,' Holmes suggested with surprising keenness.

'No, indeed I did not. However, I have engaged a room for myself in a small, but comfortable-looking hotel just behind Russell Square and my bags are awaiting me there,' Collier replied reassuringly.

'That seems to be satisfactory, although it is imperative that you maintain all necessary caution and due vigilance upon your leaving our rooms,' Holmes added gravely as he gazed dreamily towards the windows.

'You think me to be in some form of danger then, Mr Holmes?' Collier asked with surprising calmness, as I handed him a cigarette which he grabbed and lighted with much enthusiasm.

'Suffice it to say, I do think it likely,' Holmes replied in his customary inscrutable manner. He then summoned Mrs Hudson, to whom he entrusted a most urgent message before encouraging the confused Daniel Collier to conclude his reading from his father's letter.

Collier was not alone in his confusion; however, Holmes was frustratingly reticent in divulging either the nature of his message or the meaning behind his dire warning. With a resigned shrug of his shoulders Collier picked up those crumpled sheets of paper that constituted his father's final testament, for the last time.

Day ?

By the following morning the storm clouds had all but dissipated and the large deep puddles that now lay all about the camp glistened with the bright morning sunlight that heralded the day of my meeting with the 'Giant Rat'.

Their leader was held in such reverence that my companions strongly advised me to await a summons from him rather than to approach his quarters unannounced. They would inform him of my presence and the manner of my arrival in order to gauge his reaction.

This could well be some time in coming, as he had been troubled of late by bad news which had been filtering through from the mainland. Indeed, this news of further examples of British suppressions and arrests of leading figures from the Ghadar movement had been the motivation behind his decision to remove himself to the mountains in the first place. I would just have to wait.

For the first time since my arrival it was decided that I was not to be accompanied when I took my morning visit to the lakeside. I took this as a sign that I had at last gained the trust of my erstwhile captors and had, somehow, ingratiated myself into their group. This fact troubled me somewhat, for although I have never considered myself to be a jingoistic player of patriotic drums, I have always felt that I could not betray the country of my birth under any circumstances.

I decided to devote the remainder of the time that was available to me, prior to the expected summons from the 'Giant Rat', in deep meditation. I certainly had much to reflect upon as I was now questioning the true motives behind my continuing to remain within the Ghadar camp. There was now no question in my mind that I should be able to escape from there at any time of my choosing. Yet I decided to remain.

Should the opportunity arise, did I still intend to steal the beladau in the name of imperial stability? Was this purpose still important to me? More and more often my mind was going back to that day on the river when I tried to reflect upon the real difference between the lotus flower and the thorn, if indeed there was one.

I meditated upon these questions in so much depth that it was nightfall before I felt my shoulder being vigorously shaken by a lieutenant of the Ghadar. Tilat, the 'Giant Rat', was now ready to greet me!

My meditation had helped to prepare me for this meeting and how I might react to any decision that Tilat might come to. However, nothing could have really prepared me for the incredible presence that this man exuded. His simple room, which was constructed partly of canvas and partly of red-clay brick, was mutedly illuminated by two large candles in the far corner, and even the light from these was further dimmed by wreaths of smoke given off by a rack of sweet, pungent incense sticks.

The man in the centre of this sanctuary of calmness sat in the lotus position and graciously waved for me to join him in a space opposite him. With his cape and cowl removed and folded neatly behind him, he was now a man in a simple robe seated on a dusty floor. Yet the serenity that seemed to glow from every aspect of his noble countenance belied this initial impression. Seated before me he did not appear as a fearsome warrior, although he was that. Nor did he look like an undisciplined leader of revolt, although that was his reputation. This master of silat and leader of men was a truly enlightened being, seeking nothing more and nothing less than justice and freedom for his people and for his culture.

Of course I was not able to divine this much knowledge of the man merely from this initial introduction. Yet, after but a few moments of quiet conversation, I was able to reach an understanding of his nature. For reasons that I could not fully understand, Tilat had come to the conclusion that I was a man whom he could trust and empathize with. He told me of the reasons behind his past actions and even divulged much of his future plans.

You must understand, my dear boy, that under those circumstances and in the face of such an awe-inspiring presence, I could not have failed to respond in kind. As if in anticipation of my revelation Tilat reached inside a large, ornately decorated leather pouch and extracted the very icon that I had travelled so far and endured so much to seek and recover. It was almost as if he was inviting me to make off with it, if it was still my desire to do so.

I did, in fact pick up the beladau, but it was only because I wished to examine so remarkable an object under closer scrutiny. The beladau was shorter than a sword but longer than a battle knife; however its true length was hard to estimate because of the acute curvature of the blade. The handle was simply bound with red leather edged in gold. That the blade itself was fashioned from the same metal as the 'iron' pillar of Quwwatul Mosque was in little doubt. Despite its obvious age this too was displaying no indications of rust or erosion and the beautifully intricate engravings that it bore were as clear and as deep as they had been on the day that they were first cut. The fact that these engravings were also in Sanskrit with dedications to Vishnu was further proof, as if that was needed, of the beladau's original source.

Despite its undoubted beauty, Tilat assured me of its deadlier qualities and said that when used by a man of training and knowledge it was capable of decapitating a human head at a single stroke. As to whether he had ever put it to that use Tilat would not be drawn. We continued with our conversation until well into the night, during the course of which I explained at length the original motivation behind my journeys to his camp. I explained to him that, whilst I could never provide him with any form of active support, it was now no longer in my heart to betray him either.

Mercifully Tilat accepted that, although I could not even speculate as to the consequences had he not. When at last I returned to the camp for the remainder of the night, it was with the assurance that we would continue our conversation on the following day. I must confess to having looked forward to that with some lively expectancy.

Day ?

During my time in the Himalayas, apart from having been trained in the art of meditation, I was also given some initiation into the various forms of martial combats. I also discovered that the very roots of these lay within the ancient Hindu traditions. Therefore, on the following morning, I was somewhat disappointed to learn that Tilat, together with some of his men, had taken off into the highlands to confirm reports of intense Dutch activity in the foot hills of the Barisans. I had hoped to have learned more about the various forms of silat, more especially the monkey stance, known as *dangyat monyet,* about which very little is known in the west.

My companions informed me that Tilat was an undoubted master in the use of this form, which made deadly use of the palms and various weapons, including the beladau, and I had looked forward to improving my skills under Tilat's instruction.

I had to content myself, therefore, with a visit to a large wooden cage on the other side of the camp, which contained the rather unpleasant creature indigenous to Sumatra, known as the Rat Monkey.

The movements of this creature formed the basis of Tilat's own and unique martial art form. Presumably he had acquired his name and fame from his association with this small but malevolent beast. It was kept securely within its cage because of the deadly venom that its bite was supposed to possess. Its appearance was as grotesque as was its reputation. From the back or sides it was every inch a monkey, yet it was its face that belied its simian origins. It was more sharply pointed and angular than any monkey that I had ever seen or heard of and its ears sat on top of the head like a pair of tufted horns. Its demonic similarities did not end there, however, for its large, piercing black eyes sent a chill through my body, whilst its small pointed nose and its vile gaping mouth with small sharp teeth completed this diabolical vision. I could not help but shudder as it turned suddenly towards me with its talon-like hand thrust towards me, the palm raised. I was certainly most grateful for the wooden bars that constrained it as I slowly backed away.

I decided that *dangyat monyet* must be a most deadly form indeed if that creature had been its inspiration.

Day ?

The camp was full of great concern the following morning as the news that Tilat and his party had failed to return began to circulate.

Rumours that the men had been captured or even killed by the Dutch or the British armies spread like wildfire and the glare of mistrust began to return to the faces of the Ghadar whenever they looked in my direction. The conversations that we had enjoyed and the manner in which I had convinced them of my sympathy towards their cause now seemed to count for nothing. Furthermore, I seemed to have lost the freedom of movement that I had recently enjoyed. Everywhere that I went, every turn that I made, was now being shadowed by one or even two armed guards and I prayed for Tilat's safe and prompt return.

By dusk those tensions had reached fever pitch and as their looks of mistrust transformed into glares of hostility I began to regret not having made good my escape at the time when I had been presented with the best opportunity. Eventually the moment arrived when the men, now lacking strong leadership and guidance, decided to vent their fear and anger against me without waiting for their leader's return.

My harsh bonds were now re-employed and any resistance that I had offered was greeted with sharp blows to my head and body. I was on the point of being dragged away to an unknown fate when a series of loud and joyous cries went up from the guards who had been stationed around the perimeter of the camp.

Flanked by his followers and appearing to be none the worse for his protracted stay in the highlands, Tilat strode purposefully into the camp. He fiercely berated those who had been responsible for trussing me up and then demanded my immediate release. Whilst my bonds were untied both Tilat and I were offered numerous mumbled apologies for the aggressive actions taken against me. These intensified once Tilat explained that the Dutch presence had been brought about by the flight of refugees escaping from the burning city of Aceh. This was a matter of which he was convinced I was totally ignorant.

Tilat assured us that at no time had he and his men been in any danger, as they had been observing the movements of the Dutch from a safe and secluded distance. The delay in returning to camp was brought about by their having decided to take a wide and circular route and Tilat's desire to confirm that the Dutch were moving in a direction well away from the camp. He was now satisfied that this was so.

He placed a reassuring arm around my shoulder and promised to continue with our conversations the following morning.

Day ?

Tilat was as good as his word; during the course of the day the subject of our conversations turned more and more towards his unique form of silat.

I was enthralled to learn that the origins of silat could be traced back to ancient times and that its original inspiration was taken from nature itself. Various Buddhist monks, who had undertaken missionary voyages to the islands, had developed many martial arts and over 1,200 years ago introduced pentjak silat to Sumatra.

The movements of various animals were at its very core, in Tilat's case those of the Sumatran rat monkey; many of these had been individually named, poetically. As a consequence the criteria of perfection in silat are to be able to attack, but more especially to defend, with poise and with extraordinary skill.

Remarkably, silat spread and developed to such an extent that by the 1870s, when colonization was well under way, the Dutch saw fit to outlaw the use and practice of silat, as they regarded it as a significant threat to their progress. Obviously this explained the fact that much of the practice is undertaken at night time and it can also explain why so many of the movements are carried out close to the ground and in a dancelike motion. Thus may its true and deadly intention be disguised.

I therefore concluded that the current interest of the Dutch in the activities at the Temple of the Three Deities was more to do with the stories of deadly silat practitioners that were now circulating, and had nothing at all to do with Tilat's true political intentions!

During the course of various demonstrations, which Tilat

performed with some of his more senior lieutenants, the graceful, almost balletic movements were more remarkable than the deadlier intents of this form. However the latter soon became obvious, especially in the deadly palm strike, which was of particular interest to me.

Tilat refused to train me in its use as I was so sadly lacking in the essential cultural, spiritual and mental training. Then, of course, there were the physical techniques to learn: tumbling safely, kicking, blocking, all to be performed with sublime agility. Tilat could not devote sufficient time to my training whilst his group were under constant threat of discovery and destruction. Besides which, his plans for returning to India were now well advanced and his cohorts there were beseeching him to make a speedy return to rally his people.

Therefore I spent the majority of my time in meditation and in trying to acquire the martial techniques and the special movements that I had so far observed. I was particularly interested in the unusual, low-stance throws that had been adapted from the movements of small monkeys.

Some of these had evolved from the Hindu grappling techniques that I heard about years before, during my first visit to the Indian highlands and I discovered that the style, unique to western Sumatra, had been used by warriors during the early fighting against the Dutch invaders. During the course of the ensuing weeks, as a result of constant practice and hard work, I began to achieve some substantial progress.

Yet I was becoming uneasy.

On the evening that he had returned from his scouting mission, Tilat had given us assurances regarding the troop movements of the Dutch. Nonetheless, during the course of the past few days, I had noticed an increase in the number of the perimeter guards. I interrupted the course of one of our evening conversations by raising this matter, and with some concern.

At first Tilat laughed off these anxieties of mine, attributing them to my imagination. He even surmised that they might be due, in part, to the intense training that I had been subjecting myself to, of late. However, he knew me well enough by this time to realize that I was not to be put off by such explanations, and he then regarded me with a gravity that chilled me to the core.

His next action took my breath away. He picked up the beladau, ensured that it was tied securely in its pouch, then handed it to me as if he was a mother relinquishing her newborn child. The meaning behind this sacrifice of his was clear. However, he explained that it was now *imperative* that he break camp immediately and lead his men back to India, before his plans were in full readiness. The Dutch presence was heavier and more threatening than he had previously calculated and his people, encamped just south of Aceh, would lend their aid in effecting his premature exodus.

However, despite these precautions, he felt that it was imperative that the beladau did not fall into the wrong hands. He had planned an escape route for me, which could only be followed safely by a single person. He knew that I would guard the beladau with my life and that one day he would come to England to reclaim it.

He admitted that my escape would be fraught with danger, but that to remain could be more perilous still. He ignored all of my objections to his plan, for I felt that the immense trust that he was placing in me was perhaps unjustified. As if to signify that further arguments would be futile, he proceeded to wrap the beladau in the folds of his ceremonial cape; this package was further protected with some oilskin. He then outlined his plan for my escape.

The Final Day!

To my surprise Tilat confessed to me that his men had discovered my boat within just a few days of my arrival. I laughed at my inept attempts at camouflaging it. Nonetheless, his men were now preparing it with supplies and reinforcements so that it could withstand the ordeal that lay ahead. This work was now close to completion and Tilat advised me to depart immediately it was done. He could not be certain how far away the Dutch were and any delay could prove fatal.

We spent those last hours together, with Tilat divulging to me further secrets of the art of silat, of a depth and nature that he had never passed on to another living soul. We then meditated together in the spiritual tranquillity of his sanctum. During the course of this I glanced up at the man whom I now regarded as a brother, and wondered when we might next enjoy such a moment together.

Then word came that my boat was now ready to depart. There was no news of the Dutch or of their immediate whereabouts. The timing of my departure could not have been better set. Tilat and I bowed solemnly to each other and my other farewells were equally brief and formal. Last of all I ensured that the beladau was safely on board before my boat was launched once more upon the waters of Lake Toba.

As I rowed slowly away from the Temple of the Three Deities my head was throbbing as I considered the magnitude of the task and trials that now lay ahead of me. For surely was I not being entrusted with the very symbol of Hindu civilization and the talisman of Indian freedom?! Furthermore, was it not more feasible that Tilat and his men had a better chance to make good their escape than I had?

By the time I had travelled a good half-mile or so, the answer to this last question could be heard echoing towards me from the direction of the Ghadar camp. There was no mistaking the sound of volley after volley of rifle fire. Gradually the frequency of these decreased and I wondered if this was a result of there being diminished resistance from the Ghadar. Perhaps they had been successful in repelling the Dutch assault? Had Tilat made good his escape before the arrival of the Dutch?

Of course, I had no way of knowing; my first reaction to those distant sounds of battle was to turn my craft around and return to the place from where it had been launched. After I had travelled for little more than a hundred yards in that direction, I realized the futility and stupidity of my reaction. I stopped rowing again and just sat there, motionless in the water. On the one hand I felt as if I were betraying my friend; on the other, if I decided to return to his camp, I would be jeopardizing all of his aspirations and only for the sake of making an empty gesture.

I turned the boat around once more and decided to follow Tilat's directions. The sounds of rifle fire began to fade into the distance and a pillar of grey smoke rising up from the scene of battle told me that the camp of the Ghada movement was no more! However, the fate of its occupants and its leader was impossible for me to divine at this time, perhaps for ever.

So, my dear boy, I perused Tilat's detailed map and immediately struck out for the north west extremity of Lake Toba. As I have already mentioned, this great lake measures a full fifty miles from east to west. Consequently, as you might well imagine, it was several days before I was able to reach the place where Tilat had directed that I should leave the lake. By this time my energies, as well as my supplies, were at low ebb and the only thoughts that now drove me on were of the unknown fate of Tilat and of his expectations of me.

I could see from the chart that, once again, I was about to take another seat within the lap of the gods! The place that Tilat had chosen for me was the head of another waterfall. These treacherous waters would cascade down into the Alas River. Should I survive that descent, I was destined to spend another indeterminable length of time in meandering through limestone gorges and lush jungles, until the moment that the river transformed into a different kind of beast altogether.

As I was drawn ever closer to Sumatra's west coast, the river's gradient would become more extreme. Plunging rapids would follow one after another, until their force would become almost non-negotiable. At the end, when the river eventually spilt out into the Indian Ocean, I would find myself within easy reach of the coastal town of Meulaboh.

The harbour there was of such a depth as to preclude a ship of the size that might have provided me with a passage back to England. However, the occasional mail packet ship provided Meulaboh with some outside contact, and a means by which I might dispatch my papers. But, as I sat there on Lake Toba, still contemplating my next action, I decided not to entrust the beladau to such a fragile vessel. I would proceed with it, still in my precarious possession, until I should reach the more significant port of Banda Aceh.

Impossible!

I had not even given consideration to the fact that, as I still sat there deliberating with myself, the Dutch might already be in pursuit of me. Neither had I given any thought of my securing a passage for myself from Aceh without a penny or any belongings to my name! How was I to negotiate my way through the intense, continual fighting that still raged between the Dutch and the stubborn Aceh Sultanate, as I made my way towards the port? Impossible!

I was on the point of hurling Tilat's charts and instruction into the lake when I realized the high esteem in which he held me. The fact that he regarded me as capable of succeeding made the undertaking seem more than worthwhile. Should I fail? Well, I have surely lived a thousand lifetimes...!

As you have, no doubt, already realized, I have long since given up any thought of providing precise dates to these records of mine, such as they are, and I can only trust that you might understand the process of my shifting loyalties and priorities.

Should we ever have the opportunity to meet once again, my son, I trust that I might be able to look you squarely in the eye and not see pain and disappointment reflected back into my own. Perhaps Tilat's secret was supposed to have died with me all along? Perhaps the loss of the beladau will eventually lead to continuing peace and prosperity in a British ruled India? I am not certain that it is even appropriate for one such as I to weigh these lofty considerations. But such is my fate.

CHAPTER EIGHT

REFLECTIONS ON A CONSULTATION

Daniel Collier concluded reading from his father's epic journals. As he breathlessly uttered those last poignant words, he allowed the crumpled sheets to fall limply to the floor.

He sank back into his chair as the colour visibly drained away from his already grey and gaunt face and the emotion was plain to see in his eyes. I jumped up immediately and poured him out a large cognac which I handed to him together with a cigarette. He gratefully took both from me, then slowly turned towards Holmes in the hope of receiving some guidance and advice from my friend.

In this he was to be sadly disappointed. In fact, Holmes did not pass even a single comment as to the contents of the letter or its abrupt conclusion. He just stood there silently, by the window, with the stem of his unlit pipe pressed thoughtfully against his forehead.

'Mr Collier, was there anybody in Cornwall to whom you divulged your destination in London and the reasons behind your visit?' Holmes then asked suddenly and somewhat surprisingly.

Having just left his father in Sumatra, facing a precarious and unknown fate, Collier was visibly taken aback by a question that appeared so mundane and routine. He was still incapable of an immediate reply, so he lit his cigarette and took a substantial sip from his cognac.

'Apart from my landlady in St Ives, Mrs Wakeham, there was not another living soul, Mr Holmes, I assure you.'

Holmes appeared to be satisfied by Collier's answer.

'Ah, St Ives! From where you were studying those neolithic "waiting stones" that seem to interest you so,' Holmes surprisingly declared.

'Holmes,' I began cautiously, 'I do not understand. After all that we have just heard, why do you seem to be so interested in Mr Collier's landlady?'

Holmes turned sharply towards me. He appeared to be disappointed.

'Watson!' he snapped. 'Surely you would know the answer to that question even better than I. We now know that it is most unlikely that we are the only people aware of our young friend's presence here in London. That fact is of the utmost importance.'

'I am certain that Mrs Wakeham would not have betrayed my confidence. Besides, I did not divulge, even to her, the true reason behind my coming here,' Collier said defiantly.

'Very likely not; however you must understand that her apparent betrayal has, in all likelihood, been purely innocent. Why should she even think it necessary to withhold that information?' Holmes asked.

Collier shook his head slowly by way of a reply.

'Now, Mr Collier, I would suggest that you return immediately to your hotel in Russell Square, there to remain unless you receive word from either me or Doctor Watson to the contrary,' Holmes instructed sternly.

'Having now heard the conclusion to my father's letters, have you no further comments to make or advice to impart to me?' Collier asked, obviously feeling somewhat crestfallen.

'Have all of your meals sent up to your room, from where you should not remove yourself under any pretext. However, should this prove to be unavoidable you should send a note to the green cab shelter on Russell Square or to the Hansom Cab public house, on the Earl's Court road. Either of these addresses will find Dave "Gunner" King, soon enough.' By now Holmes had moved away from the window and he placed his hand reassuringly upon Collier's left shoulder.

Collier gazed up at Holmes as he asked: 'In heaven's name, Mr Holmes, who is Dave "Gunner" King?'

'Save for Watson and I, he is the only man in London into whose care I would confidently entrust your life. On many occasions he has performed a most sterling service for me; quite often this has been far above the call of duty! Do not be deceived by his bluff, round-faced geniality, for it disguises a steely resolve and the heart of a warrior. Ha! Unless I am very much mistaken he has just pulled up outside our door in a four-wheeler!' Holmes declared theatrically.

'Ah, so it was to King that you so furtively dispatched that note earlier,' I declared. 'Yet surely, even so, you go too far in claiming to know the type of vehicle in which he has now arrived? You are nowhere near the window!'

Holmes arched an eyebrow accusingly toward me. 'Evidently you did not pay sufficient attention to my notes upon the sounds and tracks made by the wheels of public vehicles and their use in the detection of crime.' I was certain Holmes had feigned his air of disappointment; however I still could not hide my embarrassment at his justified accusation.

'Do not trouble yourself, old fellow, for if the regular police force continue to ignore my various monographs, there is certainly no good reason why you should not do so also! Nevertheless, I should inform you that there is a particular four-wheeled cab that has received the nickname of the "growler". It is so called because its wheels are guarded by unusual metal rims that let out an awful grating noise whenever they pull up at the kerb. Unless I am very much mistaken, we heard such a sound a moment or two ago.'

Holmes seemed to be rather pleased with his deductions, so much so in fact, that when I escorted Collier downstairs to the waiting vehicle, I was almost disappointed to see that his prediction had been accurate. King doffed his cap cheerfully in my direction and assured me that he knew Collier's hotel very well. Notwithstanding this, Collier still seemed to be most uneasy at taking his leave of us while remaining so ignorant of Holmes's ideas and plans.

In this Collier was not alone and I mounted our stairs fully determined to extract as much information from Holmes as was possible.

To my surprise Holmes was more interested in my ideas and opinions than he was in expanding upon his own.

'So, friend Watson, I would be very interested to learn what conclusions you have arrived at, based upon all that we have experienced over the past, most extraordinary, twenty-four hours,' Holmes offered.

At that moment my eyes fell upon the clock and I realized, with some amazement, that there were barely two hours left before dawn.

'My dear fellow, would it not be more beneficial if I formulated my ideas when my mind is a good deal fresher and clearer? Have a care for the time.'

Holmes followed my gaze to the clock, but merely shrugged his shoulders.

'Have I not told you on many occasions that time is to be used as our tool and that we should never be its slave? My mind is as fresh and as active as it was twelve hours ago!' he exclaimed, smiling at my discomfiture.

'Will you not rest for just a few hours?'

As if in answer Holmes filled and lit another pipe and languidly waved me towards the door. I did not protest at this and dragged myself up the stairs, throwing myself upon my bed once I had reached my room.

Barely two hours later, despite the protests from my body, the activity in my brain was not to be quelled. My thoughts had been alternating from beladaus to 'giant rats' and back again, in rapid succession. I decided to steal down the stairs and to join my friend once more in his quest for the truth.

What I saw did not surprise me in the least. The light was still creeping from under the door and when I pushed it gently open I discovered that my friend was in a state of deep meditation. His pipe had long been abandoned to the ashtray. His pose, upon the same chair in which I had last seen him, was unusually upright, so that his unsupported head was perpendicular to the base of his spine. His legs were crossed underneath each other and his hands were folded close to his stomach I deduced, as I consequently discovered correctly from the size of the fire and the coolness of Holmes's pipe bowl, that he had been in this position from the time that I had deserted him for my bed.

From past experience I thought it best to refrain from breaking in upon my friend's spiritual quest and I made my way to my room once more. I decided that I should discover the results of his vigil once he was fully rested and recovered.

When I eventually returned to the sitting-room, I discovered, with some surprise, that a revived Holmes appeared to be considerably fresher and more alert than I was! However, he refused to discuss his experience until he had consumed at least two cups of coffee and as many cigarettes. Even then he would not divulge the results of his meditative process, merely the means by which he had achieved it.

As he spoke I suddenly realized that our conversation had come full circle and had reverted to his latest monograph, upon the subject of meditation. His efforts at outlining this to me, just moments before the arrival of the letter from Morrison, Morrison & Dodd, were now to come to fruition. Holmes explained that by concentrating upon and controlling his breathing he had been able to achieve a deep meditative state.

There were many similarities between his nature and that of Sir Michael Collier and this made it easier for him to understand the processes behind Collier's thoughts and actions. However, whenever Holmes had used this process in the past, he had been attempting to penetrate the minds of remarkable criminals. On this occasion he was trying to understand a remarkable gentleman.

At this juncture I felt compelled to protest.

'Really, Holmes! Whilst I can understand your feeling a certain affinity for a fellow free-thinking seeker after truth like Michael Collier, it is beyond belief that you should condone the actions of a man who has readily confessed to betraying his country!'

Holmes considered me in silence for a moment or two, with a wry smile that permitted a stream of smoke to issue from between his teeth.

'Ah, so that is your summation of page after heartfelt page of a man doing battle within himself. Surely you must have come to the realization that none of Collier's decisions was taken lightly. His intentions, prior to his meeting with this self-styled "Giant Rat" were clear enough, I would have thought.

'His passion for archaeology and adventure had brought him to the very bowels of political and religious revolution. Once he had become aware of the potential significance of the beladau he decided, without a moment's hesitation to reclaim this object from the clutches of the revolutionary Ghadar movement that threatened the stability of his country's Empire. Were these the motives and actions of a traitor?' Holmes asked pointedly.

'Well, no, of course not,' I replied without hesitation, although somewhat taken aback by my own admission. 'However, his subsequent actions certainly seem to throw his loyalties into question.'

'No, Watson; his subsequent actions are those of a man whose mind is in a state of turmoil. Do not forget that the letters suddenly become far more erratic and discursive and that, in reality, Collier spent many weeks, perhaps even months, in the camp of the Ghadar. During that time, while he practised and trained in the martial art of Indonesian silat, he gradually became influenced by the personality and qualities of Tilat and as a consequence Collier began to question the validity of his original motives and intentions.

'That brings us, therefore, to the fundamental question of Britain's right to rule in India. Do not reproach me, Watson, for I am fully aware that you suffered much during the Afghan campaign and that your favourite book is *The Life of General Gordon*. However we must not forget that Sir Michael Collier is undoubtedly a much travelled man who has seen and experienced a great deal that is extraordinary. Obviously he would, therefore, view these things in an entirely different perspective from our own.

'Furthermore, he has encountered many individuals who have attained a profound spiritual awareness and he has become greatly influenced by them. Let us not forget his 'lotus flower and the thorn' enigma. In that sense do we even have the right to question the morals of the man, as we sit here snugly in our rooms in Baker Street? No, our task is to try to unravel his fate after he left the shores of Lake Toba.'

Holmes had not allowed me the opportunity to respond to any of these statements of his, such had been the speed and the passion with which he had delivered them. Once he had at length paused, in order that he might put a match to another pipe, he had rendered me as breathless as he undoubtedly was. I glanced up at him, as he sat there by the window, his long sharp features silhouetted against the grey, murky dawn outside and I could see that he was greatly moved by the travails of Sir Michael Collier.

'Did your extensive meditation shed any light on the possible outcome of Collier's journeys and his subsequent fate?' I asked at last.

Holmes viewed me quizzically for a moment or two before he replied. Perhaps he was unsure as to whether my question was of a cynical or sincere nature. Evidently he was convinced of the latter.

'Sadly, it did not, although it did provide me with a profound insight into the nature of the man. I am convinced, therefore, that he would have followed Tilat's instructions to the letter and set about negotiating the Alas River. That he was successful in this endeavour we know from the fact that Collier's final letter was dispatched from Banda Aceh. As to whether Collier survived the journey from Meulaboh to Aceh is not so certain. As you might recall, it was his intention to dispatch his letter on board a packet ship from Meulaboh and it is likely that the ship's last port of call would have been Aceh.

'In his condition and with the Dutch evidently in hostile pursuit, it is highly improbable that Collier could have survived the journey from Meulaboh to Aceh; much less make it through the hostilities raging all about him as he tried to reach the quayside. No, I am afraid that Sir Michael Collier has been lost to us ... and to his son,' Holmes concluded, evidently much saddened at the thought.

I nodded solemnly in full agreement with Holmes's assessment of Collier's likely fate.

'Of course, if Collier had survived, I am of little doubt that he would have made contact with his son by now. After all, he should have arrived here several days ahead of his letters, had he lived,' I offered.

Holmes viewed me with an air of amused surprise.

'How so?'

'That is because the mail packet-ships are some of the last few vessels that still make the journey from the Far East to this country without going through the Suez Canal.' I replied.

'Why would this be?' Holmes asked, evidently amazed at the fount of knowledge that I had suddenly become. I was not altogether surprised at Holmes's apparent ignorance upon the matter. Such was the man's almost obsessive accumulating of knowledge on the subject of criminal detection that he had created a vacuum that would not allow him to concern himself with anything that was apparently irrelevant to his chosen profession.

My reply was delivered with as much pride as certainty.

'Because mail packet-ships still operate without steam and there is always a risk that a becalmed sailing vessel might obstruct the channel for days on end. Consequently they still make the journey by going around The Cape of Good Hope which adds at least a further ten days to the journey time!'

'Really? Well, Watson, you certainly scintillate at this early hour, I must say. This information of yours undoubtedly clears up a little problem of mine very nicely. As you say Collier – or anybody else, for that matter, would have arrived here several days before the letters possibly could have done. But hush! I hear a most familiar voice in the hallway downstairs. Not a word about letters, beladaus or "Giant Rats", mind you,' Holmes quietly warned me.

I nodded my confirmation just as a bedraggled Inspector Lestrade staggered into our room. I noted with some understandable relief that, on this occasion, the odious Alistair Dodd was not to be in attendance. There was an air of resigned disappointment about the hapless inspector that morning that surpassed anything that I had previously observed.

'Gentlemen,' Lestrade greeted us brusquely. 'It is certainly most heartening to witness you both so actively involved upon the matter of the *Matilda Briggs*,' Lestrade observed with unwanted sarcasm.

'Ah, you are, no doubt, referring to that trifling affair at Canary Wharf.' Holmes smiled mischievously.

'Trifling affair?' Lestrade repeated this derogatory description in a voice that can best be described as a raucous shriek. Each sinew of his scrawny neck stood out like stalks as he vented his rage and frustration. 'Have you seen this morning's papers? Have you any idea how much pressure Mr Dodd is exerting upon my superiors at the Yard? Yet still you have provided me with nothing to report. Trifling affair, indeed!'

Holmes smiled condescendingly at his erstwhile adversary and directed him towards a chair by the fire.

'Steady your nerves, Inspector, for I am certain that matters are not quite as black as you have painted them. Even now I can hear Mrs Hudson scurrying up the stairs with a tray of toast and coffee.'

Holmes immediately leapt over to the door which he flung violently open before the poor woman could have a chance to steady herself. Mrs Hudson let out a shrill nervous cry whilst she was being hustled over to the table with her tray. As she turned to leave, Holmes suddenly called her back.

'Oh, Mrs Hudson, have there been any replies to the various enquiries that you have dispatched on my behalf?' Holmes asked of her.

Our landlady shook her head solemnly.

'No, I am afraid not, Mr Holmes, save for the one that you received late yesterday evening.'

'Ah well, I suppose that one can occasionally be wide of the mark.' Holmes's response was as surprising as it had been frivolous and he unceremoniously ushered Mrs Hudson from our room.

'Well, I must say!' she could be heard protesting in the distance.

'So you can see, Inspector, that I have not been entirely inactive in your interests,' Holmes stated, still in an inappropriate, light-hearted vein.

'That might be all very well, but where are the results? There are no results!' Lestrade protested plaintively.

As Holmes heard these words his countenance suddenly assumed a far more severe appearance.

'That might be your perception of things as they stand, but evidently you have not taken up the various suggestive points that I indicated to you. For example, have you realized yet the significance of the ship's manifest? Or the shifting of Thames tides in the autumn?'

Lestrade shifted around uncomfortably in his seat without uttering a reply.

'What exactly is the significance of the tides?' I asked quietly on Lestrade's behalf.

'Ah, do not suppose for one minute that I did not observe the disparaging looks that you gave me earlier, once you had perceived my ignorance on matters concerning the Suez Canal and mail packet-ships!' Holmes said accusingly. I could not deny that his accusation was justified, but evidently I was equally unsuccessful at concealing my sense of guilt.

'I can assure you, friend Watson, that you are not the only person who has acquired relevant nautical knowledge. You might be interested to know that one of my destinations, when I left you, ostensibly to invigorate my cramped leg, was the office of the harbour master. Even though he poured me out a cup of possibly the most poisonous tea that it has ever been my misfortune to have sampled, I enjoyed a most illuminating conversation with the man.'

Holmes paused for a moment as he took a gulp from a heavily sugared cup of black coffee and lit a cigarette.

'No doubt it was he who enlightened you upon the subject of autumn tides,' I suggested with some chagrin.

I am certain that the irony in my voice was not lost on Holmes; however he now viewed Lestrade and me with a mischievous smile of triumph and he took a long luxurious draw on his cigarette.

'We discussed a good deal more than that, I can assure you,' Holmes eventually replied.

There was something in Holmes's tone of voice that prompted me to take out my notebook and pencil.

'It really has been too bad of me to have protracted things for so long. I presume that you would prefer it if I were to explain the mystery of the *Matilda Briggs* before we make our return visit to the offices of the Red Cannon shipping line in Pepys Street?' Holmes asked, somewhat unnecessarily.

'Well, of course! Yet how can you possibly claim to have solved the mystery? You have barely left our rooms in over forty-eight hours! Besides, what reason could you have for making a return visit to Pepys Street?'

Holmes shook his head dejectedly.

'Watson, Watson, you ask so many questions and make so many assumptions. You of all people should not mistake my apparent inactivity for lack of progress. Do not forget that not all of my wires have remained unanswered. For example, my enquiries of the port authorities at Port Said have revealed that young Carlo Maddelena was already a member of the crew of the *Matilda Briggs* prior to her arrival there!'

'Good heavens, Holmes, that would imply that Declan McCrory was telling us a blatant lie. But why should he wish to mislead us upon such an apparently routine matter?' I asked.

'Why indeed? However, that fact alone set into motion a chain of thought that led me to the inevitable conclusion that perhaps there were other matters upon which McCrory had not been totally honest,' Holmes replied.

'But where is any of this leading us?' an exasperated Inspector Lestrade suddenly exclaimed.

'It leads us, rather conveniently, to the three pieces of evidence that I uncovered on board the ship, which had so mysteriously eluded Scotland Yard's finest.' Lestrade turned sheepishly away as he heard this latest example of Holmes's sarcasm, a tone that Holmes delighted in whenever he might be discussing the merits of the official force.

'You have, no doubt, read and digested the contents of the *Matilda Briggs* manifest?' Holmes asked, in the manner of one who already knows the answer to his question.

'Well ... yes, of course, although there was nothing there that could possibly shed any light upon the mystery of the ship's missing crew.' Lestrade's embarrassment had been visibly heightened by this latest question from Holmes.

'Ah, so you still hold to the assumption that the crew are missing?' Holmes asked.

Lestrade laughed nervously when he heard this.

'Well, of course, what other conclusion is there to draw when a ship is found, deserted and untethered, beside a dock that she was not scheduled to put in to?'

'Perhaps that she had already been unloaded and then cut adrift by that same, supposedly missing, crew?' Holmes suggested.

This time it was Lestrade who broke into a mischievous and triumphant smile.

'Mr Holmes, while I am the first to admit that your unconventional and at times, outlandish methods have occasionally proved to be of benefit to the Yard, I fear that this latest suggestion of yours is pretty wide of the mark. For heaven's sake, man, the cargo of tea was still on board the ship when we discovered her! Besides which, all of the docks, downstream of Canary Wharf are manned throughout the night. That form of activity would not have gone unnoticed,' Lestrade concluded.

'I am not speaking of the cargo of tea, nor am I referring to those docks that are further downstream. I am now aware of the fact that at this time of year the flow turns at approximately six o'clock post meridian and therefore, the *Matilda Briggs* could not possibly have drifted into Canary Wharf had she been cut adrift downstream. She would surely have floated in the opposite direction.'

'That is all very well, but you have not, as yet, explained the nature of the evidence that you so miraculously discovered on board the ship, much less its significance.' Lestrade interrupted impatiently.

'Yes, come along, Holmes, besides which I am burning with curiosity to learn why you attach so much importance to the ship's manifest,' I encouraged.

With a deep sigh of resignation Holmes seemed to accept and recognize that the time for reticence and secrecy was now over. This was confirmed to me when Holmes took down his cherry-wood pipe and began to fill it slowly and deliberately from the Persian slipper.

'Inspector Lestrade, may I humbly suggest that you dispatch two of your more stalwart constables to the offices of the Red Cannon shipping line, in Pepys Street, without a moment's delay, there to ensure that Mr Declan McCrory remains securely within its walls until the time of our arrival. In the meantime I shall attempt to explain to you, as clearly and as succinctly as I can, my reasons for requesting you to do so.'

Such was the awe in which Lestrade held him and the respect that he accorded to Holmes's judgement that he did not hesitate for even the briefest instant; he dashed from the room to implement Holmes's instructions at once. By the time Lestrade made his breathless return to our room and threw himself back down into his chair, both he and I could sense that Holmes was now ready to lay bare the mystery of the *Matilda Briggs*.

'To begin with, I must offer to you both a thousand apologies for having maintained my silence for so long, upon this most singular affair. However, as I am sure that you both must have realized by now, I am not wont to divulge my thoughts or opinions upon a matter until I am absolutely certain of their factual grounding.

'You might remember that when I eventually emerged from the *Matilda Briggs* I had extracted three pieces of evidence from below her deserted decks. Each one of these was suggestive in itself; however, when viewed collectively they became conclusive. Furthermore, each one caused me to broaden the field of my enquiries to the extent that I dispatched wires to the port author-ities both at Port Said and Banda Aceh, in northern Sumatra.

'It will come as no surprise to you when I tell you that the first link in my chain proved to be the apparently indecipherable markings that had been etched into the ship's decking. These were no random scratchings, but rather a cleverly disguised message in the ancient Vedic language of Sanskrit. The inscriber presumably used such an obscure script because he assumed that there would be nobody aboard who could translate it, but that any educated reasoner who might come afterwards would under-stand its meaning. In that he was undoubtedly correct.

'However, before I divulge to you the significance of my trans-lation, it might mean more to you once I have explained the nature of my other discoveries. Watson, I am certain that you are about to ask me about the dust that I so painstakingly brushed into a small envelope that you obligingly held open for me. Those particles were more than mere dust, however, for they were nothing less than small grains of black peppercorns, which were to be found in more copious amounts on the lower deck.'

Holmes suddenly became aware that Lestrade and I were exchanging glances of surprised puzzlement.

'Ah, so you think my discoveries to be of nothing more than trivial significance, but you should know that black peppercorn is the principle export of Sumatra, and that not a grain comes to these shores from India! I then had to ask myself why the *Matilda Briggs* would deviate from her designated route and run the risk of becoming caught up in the violence that is engulfing Aceh, merely to take on board a cargo of black pepper. Of course, at this stage my conclusions were nothing more than mere speculation, hence my wire to Banda Aceh.

'The reply that I have received confirmed that the *Matilda Briggs* did indeed make an unscheduled call at Aceh and took on board a cargo of black pepper and a new crew member.'

'Carlo Maddalena!' I exclaimed excitedly.

'Exactly Watson, and of course my reply from Port Said has confirmed that Maddalena was already on board when the ship arrived there,' Holmes readily confirmed.

'This is all very well, but where is this information about the cabin boy getting us?' Lestrade asked, with evidently increasing frustration.

'It is getting us closer to the truth, Inspector. Despite his most youthful countenance, Maddalena was certainly no cabin boy. He was in the employ of our friend Declan McCrory and it was he who arranged for the cargo of black pepper that the crew of the *Matilda Briggs* undertook such enormous risks to procure. The question I now had to ask myself was, why run such a risk merely for the sake of such a relatively insignificant prize?

'There were two pieces of evidence that gave me my answer. My translation of the Sanskrit message was the first that presented itself, although its meaning was not immediately obvious. See here, for I have made notes of the first section:

Discover the ancient Hindu name for Sumatra

'As you know Watson, during my three-year sabbatical I spent several months in northern India and, most notably, in Tibet with the Dalai Lama. Inevitably I became acquainted with several Sanskrit phrases and a little further research now gave me my answer. The early Hindu settlers referred to Sumatra as 'The Island of Gold' and not without good reason. The intense fighting between the Dutch and the Sultanate has not been merely over its pepper and a port, even one as strategically positioned as Banda Aceh undoubtedly is! For some time now the Dutch have been aware of northern Sumatra's rich gold deposits and they have not been slow in exploiting them either. Remember, if you will, Watson, that Collier's letter frequently made mention of the presence of Dutch troops in the Toba region. I am certain that they were not merely rounding up refugees from—'

Lestrade jumped up out of chair as soon as he had heard this, in a state of great indignation.

'Who in heaven's name is Collier and what bearing does his letter have on the matter in hand? Withholding evidence is a serious offence, Mr Holmes, and I must ask you to hand this letter over at once!' Lestrade demanded, holding out his scrawny hand to receive the letter.

'All in good time, Lestrade, for it deals with another matter for which you are not yet prepared. Let me assure you, however, that any relevant information that it might contain has no bearing on the issue at hand. I can also state with certainty that if you were to act upon any anything connected with the letter's contents and its author, its recipient's life would surely be placed in serious jeopardy.'

'I should like to be the judge of that,' Lestrade answered peevishly; however when he observed the intensity in Holmes's features as he glared down at him, he immediately changed his tune.

'Of course, if it were to jeopardize our current investigation and put a man's life at risk to boot, then I would gladly delay my examination until a later time.'

'How very wise.' Holmes smiled. He pressed his forefinger to his lips as he turned away and appeared lost, for a moment or two, in deep reflection. Lestrade exchanged a puzzled glance with me, but sadly I was unable to enlighten him. However, Holmes soon broke from his reverie and continued with his remarkable analysis of the *Matilda Briggs* affair.

'The second part of my translation from the Sanskrit inscription was, in all honesty, a little more oblique.

> *... at the martyr of the wheel.*

'A little more oblique?!' I exclaimed. 'Well, Holmes, if you can make any sense of this at all, you will be deserving of the highest accolade that can be bestowed upon you.'

'That is as maybe, but you will doubtless be glad to hear that the solution to this riddle did not tax my powers of reasoning to any great extent.'

As Holmes paused to light his pipe, I glanced surreptitiously towards him and immediately confirmed that his previous statement had not been an attempt at humour and that he was completely oblivious to his display of conceit.

'Once I have explained to you the true meaning of the translation, you will see that the other elements, which you two have, so far, viewed as disconnected items of mere trivia, suddenly assume a far greater moment. A man of religion will soon inform you that "the martyr of the wheel" was none other than Saint Katherine and my visit to the harbour master revealed that the dock that bears her name is one of the few, on that stretch of the river, that has recently been expanded to accommodate cargo ships that are powered by steam.

'Of course when one views a map of our great city and then notes the proximity of St Katherine Dock to Pepys Street, well then, a point that was certainly suggestive in itself becomes immediately conclusive!'

With an air of self-satisfaction Holmes dramatically removed his pipe from his mouth and viewed Lestrade and me with a triumphant smile.

'Ah, I see that a tiny glimmer of light is now slowly illuminating the darker recesses of your reasoning.'

'Perhaps, a little,' I replied hesitantly.

'Well then, allow me to turn up the gas just a touch further for you. Watson, I trust that you remember our old friend John Douglas, also known as "Birdy" Edwards?'[1]

'Well, of course I do! He was the Pinkerton Agency man who married and then settled upon our shores after the drama of *The Valley of Fear*,' I readily confirmed.

'You should also know that he has maintained an association with many of his former collaborators and he has kindly set them to work on my behalf. I am glad to report that the results of their endeavours have confirmed my entire diagnosis.

'It would seem that Declan McCrory's investments in expanding the East Indies branch of his father's company have not, in fact, proved to be the resounding success that he would have liked us to believe. Quite the opposite, as it turns out, for his business acumen is as sadly lacking as are his subtlety and flair. His branch of the company has weakened his father's holdings, to the extent that it was all he could do to prevent his father from closing his office down altogether!

'The thought of the humiliation of returning to his father, to be branded as a failure and with his cap in hand, was more than his massive self-esteem could bear to contemplate. There had to be another way of making reparations to his company's depleted funds. Should he try to increase his tea imports? Tea is a volatile cargo at the best of times, besides which that solution would require still further investments, which he could now ill afford.

'Then his thoughts returned to the old days, back in the United States and more particularly towards a former associate of his, with whom he had maintained a regular correspondence. This man, whom Douglas's associates have identified as one Carl 'The Fox' Mandel, was a one-time drinking and gambling companion of McCrory's, who had very strong family connections with the gangs of New York's Lower East Side. It was partly the fear of his association with such a person being made known to his father, that prompted McCrory's request that he be allowed to set up the office in London in the first place.

'Mandel, in the meanwhile, became embroiled in a series of gangland killings and eventually, with the police in constant pursuit of him, he fled the United States of America to seek his fortune in the Far East. In the end he settled upon Aceh in Sumatra, where he began to provide various services of a some-what dubious nature to a band of Dutch mercenaries and soldiers of fortune that he had naturally fallen in with. I presume that by this time you can perceive the direction in which my conclusions were now moving?' Holmes asked this question somewhat hope-fully, for his discourse appeared to have taken a lot out of him and he seemed to welcome the chance to drink from his cold coffee and pause for a moment or two from his efforts.

For my part, I was glad for the chance to air my own conclu-sions upon the matter, whilst the poor inspector appeared to have been as bemused as he had been previously.

'My goodness, Holmes, the manner in which you have grap-pled with this case is, beyond a doubt, amongst your finest achievements. Each element that you have brought together, from your analysis of the tides to your reasons for dispatching those wires, rings out with the clarity of pure logical reasoning. I hope that my own understanding of your conclusions is worthy of that which I have just heard.' I cleared my throat nervously and lit a pipe of my own.

'Needless to say there are still a few aspects of the case that I am not quite clear about, but it might serve us all well if I were to make a précis of the results of the vast amount of research that you have undertaken,' I continued.

'A few aspects, you say?!' Lestrade wailed. 'I have never heard such balderdash in all my life!'

As an orchestral conductor might do, Holmes gestured Lestrade to silence with a finger to his lips, while a wave of his other hand encouraged me to proceed. At once we both complied with his directions.

'I have often observed from my case notes,' I began, 'how the analysis of a simple object, such as Doctor Mortimer's cane at the outset of the adventure of *The Hound of the Baskervilles*, has led us to extraordinary experiences. It is equally true that an apparently outlandish premise has often resulted in a comparatively mundane conclusion, such as the supposedly remarkable disappearance of Mr James Phillimore. I would say that the case of the *Matilda Briggs* certainly falls within the latter category.'

I had expected an interjection from Holmes at this point; however, when I glanced towards him I could see that his eyes were squeezed tightly shut as if he was in deep concentration. Therefore I continued without any further delay.

'I realize now why you are so unwilling to disclose your ideas before you are in full possession of the facts. My wild theorizing previously must have made me appear awfully foolish in your eyes. Plagues and pirates indeed! Nonetheless, please interrupt me if there is any aspect that I have failed to grasp.'

'Do not chastise yourself unduly, old fellow. At that time I was as much in the dark as were you,' Holmes replied with a smile.

'In brief then, the ill-judged investments of Declan McCrory plunged his father's company into dire straits. So dire, in fact, that he was forced to renew an old acquaintance from his time in New York, a ruffian whom we can now identify as one Carlo Maddalena.

'Amidst the violence and confusion that is tearing Banda Aceh apart, it was not hard for Mandel, for that is surely his correct name, to ply his nefarious trade. He and McCrory came to an agreement whereby Mandel would procure a quantity of illegal Dutch gold, while McCrory in turn would provide the means for transporting this haul from Sumatra.'

'This really is most excellent, Watson,' Holmes interrupted encouragingly. I continued, buoyed by the knowledge that I was on the right track.

'Obviously Captain Handley disguised this deviation from his intended route by conveniently losing his log. The gold was stowed in the hold, camouflaged by a cargo of black pepper and, with "Carlo", the new cabin boy safely on board, the *Matilda Briggs* set sail for Port Said.

'The subsequent events on board are harder for me to gauge. The ship obviously made its way to St Katherine Dock where the gold was unloaded and moved to Pepys Street. Once the crew was safely ashore, the ship was cut adrift, leaving its presence to be a mystery to all who found her. I presume that McCrory is now finding a buyer for his illicit gold, in the hope that his father will never discover how close his company had come to facing total financial ruin. As for the crew, well, I am certain that it would not be too difficult for McCrory to secure for them all a lucrative new berth and on a route that would keep them safely out of harm's way.'

By now Holmes was expressing his pleasure by gleefully clapping his hands.

'Well done indeed, old fellow. As for you, Inspector, I am certain that your next meeting with Mr Dodd should prove to be a somewhat less trying experience than any of the others must have been. After all, it is your diligence and investigative prowess that has saved his clients a considerable fortune in insurance and, of course, you have solved the most perplexing maritime mystery in all the annals of the sea!'

'Well I never. My diligence, my prowess? Surely Mr Holmes you must let me mention your name.' Lestrade was clearly taken aback by Holmes's apparent generosity.

'You must believe me, Lestrade, when I tell you that my reward will surely be that I never again have to clap eyes on the odious Mr Alistair Dodd! Now we must make tracks towards Pepys Street with all speed, for I am certain that your constables will be in urgent need of relief from the rage of Declan McCrory.

'Mrs Hudson, cab!'

CHAPTER NINE

SHERLOCK HOLMES AND THE IRREGULARS

By the time that we had gathered our coats and belongings together, Mrs Hudson had managed to hail the necessary cab and we were on our way back to the offices of the Red Cannon shipping line.

The narrow thoroughfares which wound their tortuous way towards the Monument, were almost impassable due to the heavy traffic, and the atmosphere on board became tense with impatience and frustration. I glanced up at Holmes and realized, with some surprise that he had not been similarly affected. He was staring at Lestrade and me with an air of superior amusement.

'Well, both of you appear to be very pleased with yourselves, I must say.' Holmes smiled.

'Mr Holmes, it is hardly surprising when you consider that thanks to your generosity, I am about to receive a most resounding slap on the back from my superiors. After all, they have been somewhat plagued by Mr Dodd and his associates and soundly rebuked for allowing you and me such a free hand in dealing with this case,' Lestrade explained with pride.

'While it is true that you will be congratulated for having unmasked and apprehended a gold-smuggler and a fraudster, I am sure you will admit that Declan McCrory is hardly as note-worthy as Moriarty or Jack the Ripper,' Holmes reminded him.

'Although, on the other hand, Holmes, he might yet prove to be the man responsible for the death of Carl Mandel,' I added on Lestrade's behalf.

Holmes shook his head emphatically.

'No, Watson, the perpetrator of that crime is a far more worthy and dangerous individual and we shall have to spread our nets a good deal further if we are to catch him,' Holmes concluded with a flourish.

'It might be as well if you acquaint the inspector with your précis of the letters of Sir Michael Collier throughout the remainder of our journey,' Holmes suggested as he closed his eyes. I immediately took out my notebook.

By the time we had eventually turned the corner into Pepys Street, I had completed my task. As I returned my notebook to its pocket my mind went back to our first visit to this address. I immediately looked towards the very spot on which I had noticed the mysterious tall man in the cape. On this occasion, however, the street was empty.

To my surprise, not one of us displayed signs of wishing to vacate our cab with any urgency as we pulled up outside our destination. I was still lost among my reminiscent thoughts. Lestrade was just sitting there with the agony of confusion etched into his intricately furrowed brow. Meanwhile, Holmes's eyes were still tightly shut as he remained in his state of deep concentration. It was almost as if the secrets of the *Matilda Briggs* and her erstwhile cabin boy were still locked somewhere within the pages of Sir Michael Collier's remarkable of letters.

Therefore, it fell to a red-faced young constable, in a state of considerable agitation, to galvanize us into action. He raced to the kerb and began to rap frantically on the door to our cab.

'Thank heavens you have come, Inspector!' the constable

breathlessly exclaimed. 'That awful American gentleman upstairs is kicking up a merry mayhem and he just won't be quiet!' The constable sidestepped smartly out of the way as Lestrade bull-ishly rushed to open the door.

'Is he now? Well, we shall soon see about that!' Lestrade snapped sharply as he barged his way towards the entrance to the building, nearly bumping into the unfortunate constable in his rush.

I was on the point of following after Lestrade when I felt a gentle restraining hand upon my arm.

'We shall give the good inspector his brief moment in the sun,' Holmes quietly suggested with a smile.

We did not need to be inside the office of the shipping magnate to experience the full wrath of the big man. His great booming voice echoed throughout the corridors and the stairwells of the entire building! As we approached the door to his room, the volume of McCrory's voice was displaying no signs of abating.

'What in heaven's name is going on here, Inspector?! Am I to be held a prisoner within the confines of my own office? This is a scandal sir, an absolute scandal!' By now McCrory had drawn himself up to his full height and he was towering over the inspector, who was visibly wilting beneath the heat of McCrory's irate barrage.

'I shall send for the American consul at once!' McCrory continued. 'You do not appear to realize exactly who you are dealing with, sir! You have not heard the last of this, I promise you!'

'Oh, I think that we have heard more than enough … from you.'

Unnoticed and unannounced Holmes had glided calmly past the bemused form of Inspector Lestrade and now stood eyeball to eyeball with the blustering American. Holmes then stabbed him in the chest with the stem of his pipe and indicated that he wanted McCrory to take to his chair.

'Well I never, how dare you sir!' McCrory's attempts at intimidating Holmes were obviously futile and his faltering voice all but tailed away to a hoarse whisper.

The manner in which Holmes's perception of the matter manifested itself in his face was so overpowering that the colour drained away from McCrory immediately. He sank down into his enormous chair, shrinking visibly as he did so.

On this occasion it was Holmes who sat commandingly on the corner of the desk, smiling malevolently down upon its owner as he lit a cigarette. Holmes offered one to his reluctant captive, whose fingers were noticeably shaking as he accepted it. Now still and totally silent, the fallen tycoon could barely lift his eyes to meet those of Sherlock Holmes.

'Oh yes, Mr Declan McCrory, we know it all!' Holmes confirmed with a solemn nod of his head.

In his turn, McCrory shook his head dejectedly; he could barely place his cigarette between his lips, so distraught was he.

'I trust that you realize that as a result of your intensive meddling, I am now to face ruin and worse still, humiliation back home. However, I cannot for the life of me understand how you came to finding me out. I was so convinced that there had been nothing that I had left uncovered or left to chance.'

If McCrory was looking to Holmes for a sign of sympathy or understanding, he was to be sorely disappointed.

'The object does not exist that can be concealed by one man, but that cannot be revealed by another,' Holmes replied enigmatically. 'Take the captain's log, for example, which you had so meticulously destroyed or, perhaps, had thrown overboard. Its very absence was more damning and raised more suspicion than anything that it might have contained!'

'Mr Holmes, you must understand from the outset that whatever else you might think of me, I am no killer. The deaths of Carl Mandel and the other members of the crew were neither a direct nor an indirect result of any of my other indiscretions—'

'Other members of the crew? Indiscretions? What is going on here, MrHolmes? This is beginning to sound like a veritable blood bath!' Lestrade shrieked in his frustration. His slap on the back was, after all, rapidly becoming a double-edged sword! I attempted to calm him down with a cigarette and a discreet assurance that Holmes would soon make the thing clear to him. In this I enjoyed only partial success, although it did allow Holmes to continue with his questioning of McCrory.

'I am well aware of that, Mr McCrory, for I have discovered enough evidence on board the ship to suggest the presence of someone who was not a member of the crew. Did Captain Handley or any of his men suggest anything to you that might aid me in identifying this stowaway?' Holmes asked unexpectedly.

'See here, Mr Holmes, my game is surely up, so I will certainly not compound my crimes by concealing anything from you that might aid you in apprehending the man who killed the members of my crew. The truth is, however, that I can add very little to what you might already know. Everything happened so quickly, you understand.

'For some inexplicable reason the presence of a stowaway was not discovered until they had begun to unload the gold at St Katherine Dock. By then, of course, it was impossible to conceal their true intentions from him and an attempt was made to apprehend him. He proved to be a most able and dangerous fighter and in the ensuing struggle he made good his escape. Captain Handley and his men delivered the gold to me as originally planned, and I have not seen them since.

'I can warn you now that to ask of me which berth I have since allocated to them, will prove to be a waste of time. The crime is surely mine alone and the crew were simply following my orders. Now, Inspector, deal with me as you will. I can assure you that any punishment that I might receive from your courts will count as nothing compared with what I would have received at home from my own people.'

With that, Lestrade moved forward to take McCrory into custody.

Unexpectedly Holmes raised his hand to call a momentary halt to proceedings.

'One moment, Inspector, and with your kind permission, of course,' Holmes purred in his most charming manner. 'I have provided you with enough evidence to try this man several times over, so I am certain that another minute or two, either way, should make little difference to you. There is just one last question that I should like to ask of Mr McCrory.'

'Under the circumstances I am hardly likely to refuse you that,' Lestrade agreed, although without entirely releasing his grip on McCrory's arm.

'There is one aspect of this business that still eludes my full understanding. I have discovered your reasons for undertaking this venture, the diversion to Sumatra, using pepper to camouflage the gold, and your choice of dock, given its location and the running of the tides. What I can not comprehend, however, are your reasons for maintaining a regular correspondence with a man like Mandel over so many years. Of course, his connections in Sumatra have subsequently proved to be invaluable to you, but you were not to realize that until only recently. Surely your bad days in New York were best left behind you, given your new set of circumstances?'

McCrory thought long and hard before making his reply.

'Sure, those days were well left behind me and they would have remained so save for one thing. Gentlemen, I must advise you all that my reasons have no bearing on the matter in hand and I would swear you all to an oath of silence upon this matter alone.'

Following a gesture from Lestrade, the two constables withdrew to the corridor outside and Lestrade and I nodded our agreement to maintaining our silence.

'I will only agree for as long as it is understood that my case should be in no way jeopardized because I have not used this information as evidence,' Lestrade added as a cautionary note.

'Very well then; the truth of the matter is that I never had any intention of maintaining an acquaintance with Mandel from the very outset. As soon as the office in London was established I realized that my friendship with a man as dangerous as Carl Mandel could prove to be a hindrance to my success over here and I did everything that was within my powers to dissociate myself from him and his way of life. However he would not be put off.

'Even once he had fled from the States he managed to maintain contact with me. Whether it were from the China Seas or even Sumatra itself, each month a new letter would surely be there on my office desk. I will not dwell for too long upon the subject matter of these letters, for reasons that will soon become obvious to you all.' McCrory paused for as long as it took for him to request another cigarette, with which I duly supplied him.

'To be blunt then, gentlemen, as a direct consequence of yet another one of my wild, hedonistic nights, in the company of Mandel and his associates, I seriously compromised a young chorus girl who went by the name of Marlene. It shames me to admit it, but I never even thought to enquire as to her surname. The issue from this violation of mine was a beautiful baby girl, whom I have never been allowed to see but whom I have been supporting from that day to this.

'Mandel rebuked and ridiculed me for taking this stance, because he and his like would simply have abandoned both Marlene and her infant girl to their fate. However, because I was a 'rich boy' and not from the Lower East Side, I had a different set of values from the others and I was, therefore, fair game. However, Mandel's plans for me did not end with a dose of mere

chiding. He decided that if I could afford to maintain my unfortunate offspring, I could equally well afford the price of Mandel's
silence.

'The full horror of his new proposal was now obvious to me.
The effects of my family discovering the results of my appalling
behaviour would lead to my ultimate destruction and Mandel
knew that, all too well! So I had no choice but to hand over a
princely sum, into his vile and filthy hands every month for the
rest of my life. The contents of Mandel's letters were the same
each time.

How is your dear father, rich boy?

'The following day a cheque would be on its way to Aceh, or
wherever he happened to be at the time, and before long the
company's funds were becoming seriously depleted. The gold
scheme was Mandel's way of securing the fruits of his blackmail
in one fell swoop and my way of throwing off his stranglehold on
me once and for all. I trust that this statement of mine will serve
adequately to answer your question, Mr Holmes?'

'More than adequately, Mr McCrory. Thank you. However, if you
are seeking either sympathy or admonishment, I can assure you that
you will not find it in this room. Perhaps one day people like you
will realize that this world and its inhabitants are much more than
merely your playthings. You may have the prisoner removed now,
Inspector Lestrade!' Holmes dramatically pronounced.

The two constables returned to do Lestrade's bidding and
before long the three of us were in the cab once more on our
return trip to Baker Street.

'Now to the real matter at hand, by which I mean, of course, the
slaying of Carl Mandel.' Holmes rubbed his hands together with
unseemly relish as he made this suggestion.

'In the absence of any available witnesses it would seem to be improbable that we can even identify this stowaway, much less apprehend him.' Lestrade shook his head disconsolately.

'Oh, Inspector, do not underestimate your powers to the extent that you would limit yourself to solving but one crime in a single day!' Then Holmes observed Lestrade's face drop as his true indebtedness to Holmes fully dawned upon him. 'You must not take my poor, mischievous, attempts at humour too cruelly, Inspector, as Watson here will most willingly attest. Now, to business.'

Our rate of progress, so far, had seemed to indicate that our return journey was to be no less dawdling than the outer one had been. Undaunted by this delay, Holmes sank back comfortably into his seat and lit a cigarette. He appeared to be positively luxuriating in the dark air of mystery that still surrounded this bizarre case.

Holmes then leant forward and balanced his elbows upon his bony knees. When he next spoke it was through a cloud of exhaled cigarette smoke.

'It really has been too bad of me to have withheld the nature of the third discovery that I made on board the *Matilda Briggs*, for this length of time,' he apologized.

The inscrutable side to Holmes's nature was never more evident than when he was on the cusp of success in a case. It had come as no surprise to me that he had taken this long to divulge the nature of a crucial piece of evidence to Lestrade, and I could only assume that he had done so now in order that he should create the maximum amount of dramatic effect with the revelation.

This attitude of his excluded any positive contribution that I might have been able to make had I been in full possession of the facts. On too many occasions I was made to feel redundant, save for my note-making and at times I had struggled to restrain the irritation and frustrations that Holmes created with his lack of regard.

More often than not, however, he would suddenly express to me the value that he attached to my help and support, and my anger would soon dissipate. This occasion would prove to be no exception and, of course, I bit my tongue.

'Oh, Watson, you must not feel aggrieved at my apparent oversight, for it does not reflect in any way upon my opinion of your abilities or worth. Rather it is, perhaps, a reflection of my own insecurities and the possibility that I might be proved wrong in my hypothesis until such time as I have explored each and every element of a problem.'

Lestrade cleared his throat to remind us of his presence.

'If you would not mind, I would like to hear of this crucial third element before we arrive at Baker Street.' Lestrade invested these last words with a most barbed and sarcastic edge.

'Oh, Inspector, we have far more to reflect upon than that, I can assure you. For example, there is that extraordinary-sounding caged animal that Collier observed within the compound of the Ghadar movement. Watson, you remember Collier's description of the creature, do you not?' This time there was no sound of exasperation to be heard coming from the direction of Lestrade, despite the bizarre nature of Holmes's question to me. Evidently and at long last, Lestrade was beginning to learn from Holmes's suggestion that he should try to expand his mind and his imagination.

I thought long and hard before I tendered a reply. I must confess that, at the time, I had attached very little importance to the beast in the cage, although I did recall that Collier's description had painted it as grotesque and demonic in appearance and repulsive and violent by nature. Apparently Tilat had based much of his silat fighting form upon the animal's movements and Collier had actually been attacked, albeit through the bars of its cage, by one of the rat monkey's peculiar movements.

Holmes appeared to have been delighted with the detail and accuracy of my recollection; he then made another suggestion:

'Perhaps you might now be able to forge a link between Mandel's dying words and Collier's description of the rat monkey?'

'Death himself has surely come for us all.'

I repeated these fateful words with a hesitant hushed reverence, while at the same time attempting to comprehend Holmes's implications.

'The most singular aspect of Mandel's dying words was undoubtedly his use of the word "himself" instead of itself as one would have expected. This certainly seems to imply that Mandel's assailant resembled, in some way, the very embodiment of death itself ...' I paused for a moment and shook my head, as if I had expected that motion to shake up and sharpen my faculties for reasoning.

'Perhaps it would help you if I now tell you of the third and final link that I discovered on board the ship. In front of the body of Carlo Mandel and below deck, amongst the remains of the black pepper, I was able to make out the traces of two extraordinarily large footprints that had clearly been impressed by straw sandals, of the type that are commonly worn in Indonesia.' Holmes paused momentarily to see if comprehension had yet dawned upon me, or Lestrade. He soon continued once he had realized that that was not to be so, just yet.

'You might remember that I examined the handrails that ran around the deck with a meticulous scrutiny that seemed to surprise you at the time?'

I nodded my affirmation.

'Well then, you might be even more surprised to learn that this examination was largely instrumental in helping me reconstruct the chain of events that led to the death of Carl Mandel. Furthermore, it confirmed for me the true identity of Mandel's killer!'

'In heaven's name, Holmes, surely you go to far this time!'

'On the contrary, Watson, for surely the sandal-print on the handrail confirms the method of the killer's escape, and the bloodstain, which was smudged into the wood close by, means that Mandel was not the killer's only victim! As to his identity, well surely it is obvious now—'

'Tilat, the Giant Rat of Sumatra!' I exclaimed. 'Although the chain of events that led to his slaying members of the crew of the Matilda Briggs, are as yet unclear to me.' I added tamely.

At this juncture, Lestrade held up his hand, as if in a gesture of surrender and despair.

'Mr Holmes, are you asking me to believe that the leader of a revolutionary movement, whose place of refuge, on the island of Sumatra, suddenly comes under attack from the Dutch army, somehow miraculously appears in London and starts killing the crew of a merchant ship?

'While I will readily admit to owing you a huge debt of thanks for handing Declan McCrory to me on a plate, I cannot contemplate, even for an instant, taking this theory of yours back to the Yard without risking both severe censure and possible dismissal,' Lestrade added defiantly.

'Ah, but clearly, you do not appreciate the true measure of the importance and reverence that Tilat and his people had attached to the talismanic beladau. After all, when he was in fear of his imminent destruction, did not Tilat entrust his most valued possession to the only person he thought had a chance of surviving the Dutch attack, Sir Michael Collier?

'Having survived that attack do you not think it more than likely that the very first thing that Tilat would do would be to try to reclaim the very symbol of his people's struggle for freedom? Do not forget that he had collaborators waiting to help him in Aceh and it is not unreasonable to suppose that a man of his extraordinary abilities would have had little difficulty in stowing himself away on board the fastest ship available that would take him to England.

'He was convinced that Collier would have survived his ordeal and upon reclaiming the beladau, Tilat had every intention of returning to India and using it to rally his people behind it once again. Unfortunately for him, when the gold was eventually offloaded at St Katherine Dock, he was discovered in the hold and during the course of the ensuing mayhem he was forced to kill in order to make good his escape over the side.

'The last of his victims was, obviously, the odious Carl Mandel, a man whose unlamentable loss should not weigh too heavily on Tilat's conscience. You can, no doubt, imagine Mandel's state of mind as he lay there on the deck, gazing up at Tilat, disguised in his cape and mask, every inch the "Giant Rat of Sumatra" and a vision of "Death himself". Indeed, it is possible that he was not even fully aware of where the blow that killed him came from, as Tilat's iron palm strike would have been both swift and subtle.'

I shook my head slowly in disbelief and Lestrade emitted a long slow whistle in both amazement and incredulity.

'My my, Holmes; as usual you have explained everything with your customary clarity and vision.' I sighed.

'I must say, Mr Holmes, that you certainly seem to have identified our killer with a flawless piece of detective work although, perhaps, you employed just a small touch of intuition,' Lestrade offered.

'I think that you will find that it was meditation rather than intuition, Inspector,' I corrected. 'Sherlock Holmes never guesses.' I saw Holmes smile proudly at the manner in which I had set Lestrade right.

'Well, I am sure that I do not know about such things. We adopt more mundane and practical methods at the Yard. However there is still the small matter of Tilat's current whereabouts to consider. If the purpose behind his illicit journey to London was to reclaim this beladau thing from Sir Michael Collier, then I am afraid he has been very much let down.

'Clearly there remains nothing to detain him here any longer and therefore any hopes that we might have had of apprehending him have been thwarted,' Lestrade complained.

'Not so, Inspector. You are forgetting the presence in London of Collier's son Daniel. If, as we suspect, Tilat is aware of his existence also, then surely he will not quit these shores until he has at least tried to obtain the beladau from him.'

'Yet you would think that someone of such a distinctive appearance would not have gone these many days without having been noticed at least once?' Lestrade persisted.

'Ah, well, there we need to plead for a little tolerance on your part. You see, your previous statement was not, strictly speaking, a totally accurate one.' Holmes turned away warily, in anticipation of Lestrade's inevitable reaction.

'You mean to tell me that you have seen this man, someone who is strongly linked to at least one killing, without having reported this to the authorities?'

'Watson, perhaps you would care to explain to the good inspector the exact circumstances of your encounters with the man in the crimson robe?' Holmes suggested as he nonchalantly lit another cigarette.

'You must understand, Lestrade, that at the time I did not fully understand the true significance of the man's presence here. Furthermore, I was not even certain that I could trust my own eyes, amidst the murky swirling mists of a grey early morning.' Lestrade did not appear to be totally convinced and so I went on to describe every detail of the two occasions that I had observed the man we now knew to be Tilat, or the 'Giant Rat of Sumatra'.

'Well then, if that is the case, we must do everything within our power to find and apprehend this individual, before anybody else is killed,' Lestrade stated boldly.

'You should be glad to hear, therefore, that I have already taken steps that will help to bring this about,' Holmes replied. 'There is little doubt in my mind that Tilat is already aware of Daniel Collier's visit to our rooms, so I suspect that any attempts by Watson or by me at tracking him down will meet with little or no success. Equally and with all due respect, you and your men will meet with similar failure, given the ham-fisted manner in which you go about your business.'

'Thank you very much, Mr Holmes,' Lestrade responded sarcastically. 'I am sure that my colleagues at the Yard will appreciate your high opinion of their efforts. Nevertheless, your assessment seems to have left us with very few options—'

'Holmes! You have sent for the Irregulars!' I suddenly concluded enthusiastically.

As if I needed any confirmation of my statement, as we turned the corner into Baker Street I could see a small group of around four or five street 'Arabs' who had gathered in front of the entrance to 221B.

Lestrade laughed as soon as he realized my reaction to the sight of the boys.

'Well, I must say, that little lot will be a fine match for a trained killer like Tilat!'

Holmes rebuked Lestrade's ridicule with his sternest of glares.

'You must realize that these innocuous-looking little urchins know their way about the docklands better than any man and should have little or no difficulty in ferreting out our quarry – if he is still to be found, that is. Furthermore, they will be able to accomplish this task without Tilat's being aware that he has been detected, therefore we need have no fears that he will take premature flight.

'You were not present at the conclusion of *The Sign of Four* affair, but you should be aware of their effectiveness in not only finding Jonathan Small, but also his proposed means of escape!

They can infiltrate any backstreet or backwater and remain invisible by virtue of their being so very commonplace. But wait! They seem to be without their leader.'

I should mention here that their self-styled commander, who went by the name of Wiggins, no doubt achieved this position of power by virtue of his most singular appearance. He stood at well over a head above his peers and his extraordinary height was accentuated by a frame that can best described as skeletal.

The boys became quite excited when they recognized us through the cab window, no doubt anticipating a task being set for them by Holmes, for which they would be suitably recompensed. Sadly their bare survival upon the streets was only made possible by their abilities as pickpockets and other forms of minor larceny. But where was Wiggins? This was the first question that we asked of them as we pulled up at the kerb.

The oldest boy of the group stood forward.

'Oh Mr 'Olmes, 'e remembered 'ow upset your landlady was the last time we all thumped upstairs, so 'e's waiting for you in your room on 'is own.'

Holmes patted him gently upon the head and smiled down upon them all with surprising fondness as he climbed out of the cab.

'Good boys,' Holmes said quietly, before turning back to speak to Lestrade.

'I expect to allay your scepticism within forty-eight hours and I will call for you once the chase is about to begin,' he informed the inspector. 'In the meantime I suggest that you dispatch your best man to Daniel Collier's hotel without a moment's delay. Although I have furnished him with the services of a most stalwart ally of mine, should the need arise, I would say that at this stage of the game we would do well to employ every due precaution.'

'I have just the man for the job and he shall be on his way to

Russell Square from the minute that I arrive back at the Yard,' Lestrade confirmed. 'I shall wait at my desk for your call.'

'Scotland Yard, cabby, and do not spare the horse!' he called out as he rapped sharply upon the roof of the cab.

Holmes and I sprinted up the stairs to spare Mrs Hudson even one more moment of anxiety.

CHAPTER TEN

On the Trail of the Giant Rat

When we reached our room we found Wiggins perched rather uncomfortably on the edge of a wooden chair while our vigilant landlady stood sternly and watchfully over him. She was unaware that, despite their appearance, the 'Irregulars' lived by a certain code that would preclude them from stealing from someone like Holmes, who would always treat them with the utmost respect.

It was impossible to say who was the more relieved by the sight of our sudden arrival, Wiggins or the landlady. It was easier to gauge who was the most vocal in expressing it.

'I do not know, Mr Holmes, but as if some of your clients are not curious enough, for you to invite boys like this to my house is the last straw! I have not taken my eyes off of the wretch for one second.' Mrs Hudson shook her head despairingly as she tut-tutted repeatedly.

'Thank you for your concern, Mrs Hudson, but I can assure you that everything is quite safe in the hands of young Wiggins here,' Holmes cheerily explained.

'Oh yes, indeed sir, quite safe I can assure you.' The young fellow jumped up from his chair and displayed that his grimy hands were quite empty.

'Well, I do not know.' Mrs Hudson was still complaining even while Holmes was gently ushering her out of the room.

'Goodbye, Mrs Hudson!' He smiled as he closed the door behind her.

The tall scarecrow of a lad who stood before us repeatedly pulled his unwashed, unruly hair away from a face that was stained and roughened by the soot and filth that pervaded the streets on which he lived. He was not alone, of course, for the saddest indictment of our times is the copious number of his like who eke out the barest existence upon the darkened streets where the majority of London's inhabitants never dare to walk.

Wiggins and the other Irregulars were fortunate indeed in having earned the trust and the respect of one such as Sherlock Holmes. On more than one occasion Holmes had employed their knowledge of the streets and their ability to penetrate the very underbelly of London without detection or suspicion, to help bring a criminal to justice. They had never let him down and each success had always brought to them the handsome reward that Holmes had promised them.

Small wonder then that Wiggins now stood to attention in front of Holmes as he eagerly awaited his latest set of instructions.

'Mighty glad to get your latest summons, we are, Mr 'Olmes. Me and the lads are ready for whatever you want to throw our way,' Wiggins offered eagerly.

'How does a florin a man sound to you and double that to whoever is fortunate enough to land the fish.'

'Cor blimey, Mr 'Olmes, that sounds right 'andsome to me. What we got to do for that, swim the bloomin' Channel?' Wiggins asked. As he rubbed his hands together in anticipation, his threadbare mittens shed some soiled decaying wool on to our floor.

'Nothing as daunting as that, I can assure you, although it will involve you scouring the docklands once again. The Canary

Wharf area, to be more precise. Have you heard of the steam clipper the *Matilda Briggs*?'

''Course I 'ave. She's the bloomin' ship where all the crew went missin', ain't she?'

'Well, not quite all, but she also had a stowaway on board who should prove to be far easier to find than the rest. You will be looking for a man fully six feet five inches in height with a strong, upright bearing. He was last seen wearing a pair of straw oriental sandals and a long crimson – or dark red – robe and mask.'

'I know what crimson means, Mr 'Olmes. Just 'cause I don't speak the same as you don't mean I don't know nothin'.' Wiggins appeared to be genuinely hurt by Holmes's assumption.

'Wiggins, I sincerely apologize to you. Now, do you think that you and your men will be able to find such a man for me?'

'If we can't then 'e don't exist, Mr 'Olmes.' Wiggins emphatically replied and Holmes and I could not repress a smile at his self-confidence.

'That is not all, however. For the price of a new pair of mittens for each of you, I need to discover when he intends to depart and his proposed means of doing so. Do not forget that he will be returning to the Far East, so that might help you in finding the ship. Now remember, Wiggins, you are not to take any unnecessary risks. Be as discreet as ever and keep yourselves safe at all times.'

'Don't worry 'bout us, Mr 'Olmes we'll be as safe as 'ouses and we'll find your man in next to no time!'

'Excellent! Now, call your friends upstairs and I will ask Mrs Hudson to bring us all some nice hot muffins.' Holmes rubbed his hands together expectantly, then added, 'Do not forget, new mittens, Wiggins, not a noggin of gin!'

'No mistake, Mr 'Olmes. It's going to be a hard winter, they reckon.'

It fell to me to try to persuade Mrs Hudson to supply muffins for six and once she had relented, Wiggins and the other Irregulars departed with warm full bellies and the promise of riches and mittens should they pull off another job for Sherlock Holmes. We could hear their loud chattering until they had fully reached the Marylebone Road!

Once order had been restored Holmes and I pulled our chairs up to the fire and lit our pipes.

'I sincerely hope that you have not given the Irregulars too much to chew upon, this time,' I ventured.

'I would certainly rather entrust this task to Wiggins and his boys than to Lestrade and his men. Besides, their safety lies in the fact that Tilat will not be looking for them, nor will he be surprised if he sees them,' Holmes replied.

'Whilst that is undoubtedly true, it is also accurate to say that Tilat has already proved himself to be a most dangerous man and they are, after all, only boys,' I reminded him.

'Watson, you are forgetting that Tilat only killed in self-defence and that his only motive for being here in the first place is to retrieve his sacred beladau. I am certain that if we can successfully maintain Daniel Collier's safety it will not be too long before Tilat will have to show his hand. Once he does, of course, he will show himself to the Irregulars and we shall have him!'

As usual I could not fault any of Holmes's reasoning and we both sank into a relaxed silence. After a light supper followed by a cognac and cigar, I could sense that Holmes was falling into one of his more reflective moods and that he could not be drawn into a conversation upon any subject, not even upon the matter at hand. I decided to withdraw to my room with a good book and the remainder of my drink.

After about an hour or so I could feel my tired eyes gradually closing. So I put down my book and decided to look in on Holmes before retiring for the night. I was not surprised to find that he had now abandoned his cigar to the ashtray and that his cognac remained untouched. I was not surprised to see that he was now seated in his meditation posture and that he obviously had every intention of remaining there for the entire night.

However I was most disturbed to see that on this occasion his meditation was proving to be a most unsettling experience for him. He was sweating profusely, his lips were discoloured by dehydration and he seemed to be unable to remain still. He also appeared to be talking to himself under his breath. He repeated the same phrase over and over again, almost as if he were recounting a perverse form of mantra.

'I cannot penetrate the veil, I cannot penetrate the veil!' The longer this repetition continued the louder and more violent it appeared to become. Indeed, it was all that I could do to refrain from doing the unthinkable. To break in upon Holmes's meditation was something that I would not ordinarily consider doing, even for an instant, but it was rapidly becoming the safest, perhaps the only option, especially under these circumstances.

I found myself gripping Holmes, firmly by his shoulders, shaking him back and forth repeatedly, in the hope that I might rouse him from his strange trance. In this I was only partially successful at first. Holmes reacted by flailing his arms around wildly and violently in an incoherent attempt to break my grip upon him. But I would not be put off, and after a short while his arms' frantic movements began to slow down and he opened his red and bleary eyes.

I was shocked to observe that at first, he did not appear to recognize me; he just stared blankly ahead of him into an ineffable space. However once he did become aware of my presence he appeared to be horrified by his own behaviour.

'Oh, my dear fellow, I must offer to you a thousand apologies for this sorry show of mine. I should tell you, however, that I am now certain that Tilat will not depart until he has found Daniel

Collier and retrieved the beladau from him, although with no violent intent.'

'Well I am certainly relieved to hear that,' I confirmed. 'However I am more concerned about your health. How do you feel now, after such a harrowing experience?'

Holmes smiled at my enquiry as he helped himself to the cigarette that I now offered to him. As he put a flame to it I could not fail to notice a slight hand tremor that caused him to miss the tip.

'I shall soon be well, old fellow, I can assure you. Do not concern yourself, for not every experience of meditation is a calming or an enlightening one.'

'Are you able to discuss the veil, which seemed to disturb you so much?" I asked somewhat tentatively.

'There is really very little to discuss, for the reference was purely metaphoric. So much is now clear to me and yet there is one small cloud that simply will not be dispersed. However I am certain that its meaning will prove to be of very little significance and that our first concern is to be prepared once we receive word from Wiggins and his gang, or perhaps from Russell Square.' Holmes's last sentence tailed off into a long deep yawn and I was pleasantly surprised to see how willing he was to retire to his room for the night. I needed very little persuasion to follow suit.

When I came down for breakfast on the following morning, I was more than a little taken aback when I realized that Holmes had yet to emerge from his room. Under normal circumstances this would not have seemed to be too unusual, for Holmes was wont to keep most bohemian hours whenever he was not gainfully employed.

On this occasion, however, he was not only fully occupied, but this most taxing of cases was now close to its potentially exhilarating climax. To find him still beneath his covers in view of the current state of affairs was totally unheard of and I raised this point once he had eventually joined me at the breakfast table. His uncharacteristic behaviour continued as he made short work of a delicious plateful of devilled kidneys and eggs.

'You should not be too astonished, Doctor, for this is my first full meal for over seventy-two hours and I have barely slept a wink for two whole days! Nevertheless, it is true to say that last night's mysterious experience has undoubtedly taken its toll, even upon a resilient constitution such as mine,' Holmes explained between mouthfuls. 'I presume that there has been no word from Wiggins or from Russell Square?' Holmes added somewhat futilely, knowing full well that had there been we would not be wasting our time around a meal table, and so I answered him.

'Well, I suppose that my expectations were somewhat premature,' Holmes commented with surprising nonchalance as he lit his first cigarette of the day.

There was little doubt in my mind that a lot more had occurred to Holmes on the previous night than he was now willing to divulge to me, and I had to take it on faith that whatever it had been was not pertinent to the conclusion of the case.

Leaving Holmes to his own devices, I set out for the morning papers. On my way to Simon's stand I could not help but shift my gaze towards the corner with the Marylebone Road, on which I had seen the caped stranger for the second time. On this occasion the thoroughfare was teaming with traffic of every description. Businessmen on their way to the Metropolitan railway station, resplendent in their shiny tall hats and overcoats, barrow boys threading their way through the bustle and young maids running errands for their mistresses. However, there was not one tall stranger in his cape to be seen!

One glance at the headlines was enough to alter the tempo of my gait and I collided with at least two of these passers-by as I careered back to our rooms to show them to Holmes.

A Triumph as Scotland Yard's Finest, Inspector Lestrade, solves the Mystery of the Matilda Briggs

---

Holmes snatched the paper from me with an alarming display of impatience and he held out its sheets to the limit of his outstretched arms. The article, which was placed at the top of page two of the Telegraph, was not a particularly long one and did not include even one detail of Holmes's analysis.

'Ha! Scotland Yard's finest, indeed!' Holmes exclaimed, and he was barely able to disguise his ridicule. 'Well, this is indeed a sorry indictment of the current state of our capital's constabulary, I must say.'

'Is that all you have to say about it?' I asked. 'Does it not concern you at all that your name is not mentioned even once?'

'Watson, I can assure you that those lamentably romantic yarns of which you are so misguidedly proud have provided me with significantly more fame than I could possibly know what to do with.'

'Holmes, that is both undignified and unjust of you!' I protested. 'After all, I feel that my writing has always done you full justice.'

'That is as maybe, but what of the logic and the pure rational reasoning behind my investigations? In your efforts to please your ignorant public with unnecessary prose and hyperbole you have clouded the real issues. What might once have been informative scientific exercises in the processes of deduction have been blown up into a series of ham-fisted pot-boilers! You have surely wasted a unique opportunity,' Holmes declared ruefully and not without a little asperity.

'I shall excuse your boorish behaviour on the grounds that you have grown impatient and irritable while you await news from Wiggins and his gang,' I replied. 'However I shall not just sit here and allow myself to be unreasonably maligned. I am going out for a walk!'

As I made for my coat and hat, Holmes turned away and dismissed me with an airy flick of his fingers. I made sure that the door closed behind me with a most resounding thud.

By the time that I had stepped out on to the street once more, I found that the early-morning turmoil had lessoned somewhat and that my passage was to be considerably clearer. I turned into Marylebone Road once again and began moving instinctively in an easterly direction. I passed the magnificent waxworks exhibition of Madame Tussauds and before long, as I reached the entrance to the park, I realized that I was being drawn inexorably towards Russell Square!

I was not certain as to the reason for this diversion of mine or even what my expectations would be once I reached Collier's hotel. Yet as I passed the turning into Gower Street I was suddenly consumed with a sense of dread that would not be allayed, and I turned away from my intended path. I decided there and then that it would better for me not to complete my journey; instead I would explore the Church of Christ the King, in Gordon Square, a building that had always held a certain fascination for me.

It was then that I caught a fleeting glimpse of a familiar figure in a crimson cape!

On this occasion there was little doubt in my mind as to the identity of this mysterious apparition and at once I took up the chase. I also committed the fundamental error of calling after him as I did so and, of course he immediately took flight. Being a highly skilled warrior, my quarry proved to be remarkably fleet of foot and I soon found myself losing ground to him.

I realized at once that there was no reasonable chance of my actually catching him, yet I remained resolute in my pursuit. Woburn Square turned into Woburn Place and at each corner that we turned I could not catch more that a tantalizing image of the tail of the cape as it disappeared into the next street. At last and inevitably I did arrive at my original destination, now breathless and perspiring freely. Not surprisingly, the object of my quest was nowhere to be seen.

As soon as I had fully recovered my composure I crossed the road towards Collier's hotel and I immediately recognized Sergeant Rutherford, Lestrade's 'best man', who had been left to stand vigil on the steps outside. I questioned him rigorously regarding the comings and goings at the hotel entrance that morning and he confirmed that he had not noticed anyone untoward within a hundred yards of the place. He also informed me that the rear entrance was used exclusively for tradesmen's deliveries and that it remained under lock and key when not in use.

I left the officer to his duties and smoked a cigarette while I weighed up my options. There was little doubt in my mind that my futile pursuit of Tilat would have affected Holmes's plans in one of two ways. Tilat would now be aware that any attempt that he might now make to meet Collier would no longer remain undetected. He would surely abandon his plans for recovering the beladau and go to ground before returning once more to his people in the East. All would be lost and I was certain that Holmes would be inconsolable.

On a more positive note, there was a realistic chance that Tilat would now become desperate and throw caution to the wind. This, of course, would greatly increase the chances of the Irregulars coming across Tilat's bolt hole and I would need to return to Baker Street before we received word from them.

I threw my cigarette to the gutter and decided to satisfy myself as to Collier's welfare before taking a cab back to our rooms. I was gratified to note that due vigilance was being observed by the concierge, and that I was not allowed to mount the stairs until Rutherford had confirmed my identity to him. Collier's room was situated on a secluded corridor on the second floor. The only window that serviced the corridor was tiny and secure and I realized that Collier had chosen well.

Collier called out in order to confirm that it was safe to let me in, and appeared most relieved to see me once he had eventually turned the key to his door. I was shocked to note the effect that this period of seclusion had had on his appearance. He was clearly in need of a shave and a hairbrush. An untouched tray of food and his emaciated grey countenance told of at least one day without food. An ashtray full of the ends of his distinctive cheroots informed me of the manner in which he had spent his time. Of course this was confirmed by the dense fog of smoke that now pervaded the room. This was made worse by the windows being left closed and locked, as a precaution.

'Oh Doctor, perhaps you can let me know for how much longer I am to remain incarcerated?' he exclaimed, pulling upon my coat collar as he beseeched me for information. 'Sergeant Rutherford has been very kind and efficient, but he is hardly very forthcoming.'

'My dear fellow, it shall not be for much longer, I can assure you. Mr Holmes's plans are now well progressed and he is confident that the danger that now threatens you will soon be removed for ever.' I placed a reassuring hand upon the young man's shoulders, to help to confirm my statement. I then informed him of the events that had taken place at the shipping office and the involvement of the Baker Street Irregulars without revealing anything that might have disturbed him further.

'Thank you, Doctor.' Collier smiled weakly. 'Please inform Mr Holmes that whatever the nature of the dark forces that are abroad, I would like to be present at the death.'

I was greatly moved by the intensity and the sincerity of Collier's request.

'I believe that you have earned at least that much,' I assured him. 'You should be fully prepared for a call from Sergeant Rutherford, for from the moment that it comes there will be little or no time to lose!'

With that I shook him by the hand and took my leave. 'Gunner' King ensured me a speedy return to 221B, but when I burst in upon Holmes I found him in a most melancholy frame of mind. I would not have normally expected any form of an apology from my proud friend; a wave of his hand towards the table by the side of my chair was the nearest that I was ever likely to receive from him.

I followed his gesture and discovered that the table contained a glass of my favourite port and one of his finest cigars. It seemed as if he had not moved a jot throughout my absence, for he still sat with his back to the door. He turned now, slowly and diffidently towards me, so that he could witness my reaction. I could not help but smile at his attempt at reconciliation and he knew it.

'Ha, Watson! I had hoped that my humble offering would tempt you into returning to the fold.'

'It was very kind of you,' I grudgingly conceded.

Realizing that I was not to be so easily won over, he ran across to me and offered to put a light to my cigar.

'Watson, you should not be too dismayed at my harsh treatment of your literary skills. After all, as you so correctly observed, my mood has not been best served by this interminable waiting. Besides which, your work has much merit in it and you should remember that I certainly have no proficiency in the skills of a scribe.'

With these words the whole matter was duly dismissed from Holmes's mind and he set to making his plans preparatory to receiving word from the Irregulars. Before he was able to proceed further, however, I thought it best to inform him without delay of my encounter, on the way to Russell Square and the state of affairs at Collier's hotel. I fully expected to receive another vitriolic condemnation for having placed his plans in jeopardy, but again I was to be pleasantly surprised.

'Well, well, so it fell to you, friend Watson, to accelerate the turning of the wheels. I should not be at all surprised if we were to receive word from Wiggins before the morning.' Without another word Holmes picked up his violin and treated me to a delightful rendition of Bruch's sublime concerto. Under the circumstances it seemed miraculous to me that he was able to do so without hitting a single false note.

By the time that the supper things had been removed all thoughts of Bruch had been long forgotten and Holmes began to pace the room once more as his frustration steadily increased. I tried to distract myself from his angst by diving into the morning papers once again. However, after an hour or so had passed and I had had little success, I found that the effects of the fire and my port were gradually luring me to my room. I decided to abandon Holmes to his prowling and his pipes and a short while later I fell into a wonderful sound sleep.

My consciousness had neither the time nor the inclination for troubling thoughts or dreams and I was only disturbed from my slumber when a vicelike grip fastened itself upon my left shoulder. With a groan I rolled myself slowly over on to my back, to find Holmes glaring down upon me with the glint of excitement shining from his tired eyes. He could barely suppress a smile of anticipation at the thought of the imminent conclusion to the case.

'Watson, our journey is nearly over. Do stir yourself, for Lestrade and "Gunner" King are awaiting us in a cab on the street below!'

'Holmes, why is it that the defining moment in every case

seems to occur at half past four in the morning?' I asked wearily, once I had glanced at my clock.

'Do not concern yourself with such things, for time is of the very essence,' Holmes reminded me as he left my room.

A moment later, before I had even pulled back my blanket, he was back and calling through the door.

'Do not forget to take all precautions.' By which he was prompting me to ensure that my loaded army revolver was with me when I left the room. My years of army life had trained me for preparation at a moment's notice. Consequently I was dressed and my revolver was loaded and primed for action in less than four minutes.

I patted my coat pocket for reassurance as I closed my bedroom door behind me.

CHAPTER ELEVEN

THE MAN IN THE CRIMSON ROBE

By the time that I had reached the cab, King already had his whip poised above his head and we set off at once at a cracking gallop towards Daniel Collier's hotel.

Young Wiggins was perched on a seat opposite to that of Holmes and a zealous Lestrade made up the quartet. As I shuffled into my seat Wiggins was in the process of describing to Holmes the lengths that he and the other Irregulars had gone to in tracking down the elusive man from Sumatra.

'It weren't easy, Mr 'Olmes, I can tell yer. Me an' the lads must 'ave been up and down the water's edge a dozen times or more before we find 'im. Them docklands ain't no walk in the park, in the dead of night, neither.

'But we put the word about, you see, and when young Corky 'eard of a run-down old ware'ouse down near the Canary docks he got as close as he dare so he could get a good dekko. From what you told me about his get-up, Corky knew 'e ain't made no mistake!'

By the time that Wiggins had finished his report, Holmes was chuckling to himself at Wiggins's notion that he would need persuasion to hand over the proper wage for the job.

'You have all done exceptionally well; however, I will still require you to point out to us the exact situation of the warehouse before we deposit you at a safe distance from whatever might occur.' As he spoke, Holmes began to count out the coins into the extended and eager palm of the young street Arab.

'That's very generous of you, Mr 'olmes. The lads will be pleased and no mistake.'

'Do not forget your promise that the bonus is to spent on new mittens for you all.' Holmes smiled.

'Mr 'Olmes,' Wiggins responded in a tone of mock indignation, 'as if me and the lads would squander it on anything else!'

Holmes cast him a momentary look of suspicion before turning his attention to the man from Scotland Yard.

'Now, Inspector, are you able to confirm that all of your arrangements have been set in motion?'

'I am, Mr Holmes. I will have a dozen men or more cordoning off the entire area, in case this fellow should slip past us, and I have arranged for two of these new police steam launches to patrol the waters to ensure that he does not make it to the *Bellerophon.*'

I should point out here that, just prior to my entering the cab Wiggins had been explaining how he had also ascertained that Tilat had arranged a passage for himself aboard a small Greek schooner, the *Bellerophon,* which was scheduled to depart for the East at first light that very morning! Evidently my near confrontation, with Tilat had brought events forward considerably and 'Gunner' King seemed to be well aware of the urgency, if his current rate of progress was anything to judge by.

'You have done well, Inspector. Every eventuality has now been anticipated and I am certain that this affair can be brought to a satisfactory conclusion on this very morning!' Holmes enthusiastically declared.

We arrived at Collier's hotel in what, I am certain, was record time. We were gratified to see that the dishevelled young archaeologist met us at the cab most promptly, with the ever vigilant Sergeant Rutherford in a close attendance. With our party now complete, we set off for Canary Wharf!

The deserted streets were bathed in the cold grey light of a dozen gas lamps, which gradually became rarer and dimmer as we drew ever closer to the river. The echoes from the horse's hoofs seemed to resound throughout every corner of the city and we soon realized that the element of surprise would surely be lost unless we slowed the speed of our approach. King was not unmindful of this and as we slowed to a walk I could sense the growing tension amongst the occupants of the cab.

Lestrade stared blindly ahead of him, unmindful of his surroundings as his mind played out every possible eventuality that he could imagine. Judging by the forlorn look on his face, none of them was good. For his part, Collier just seemed to be glad that he was at last able to escape the claustrophobic confines of his room. He was fired by the prospect of some excitement and he was constantly twisting the barrel of his revolver, as if there was a chance that he had missed a bullet on the last occasion he had checked them.

Wiggins was incessantly straining his neck through the window, so that he was able to give us as much warning as he could, before we came too close to Tilat's hideout. Rutherford was every inch the resolute professional. He moved not a jot and his large, impassive face did not betray a single thought or emotion.

Holmes sat quite still, with his eyes tightly shut. A strange enigmatic smile, which occasionally touched his lips, seemed to indicate that the thought of the imminent confrontation had calmed his fraught nerves. All the while he was softly humming a few chords from the Bruch concerto that he had treated me to earlier.

The distant muffled groan of a ship's fog horn warned us that we were now close to the water. Holmes's eyes suddenly sprang open, as if they had suddenly been released. He immediately offered cigarettes to each one of us, even to the boy, and I, for one, accepted mine with an unbecoming fervour. After all, a man can only get so much comfort from a cold hunk of metal in his pocket!

A thick dawn fog, which was flirting with the surface of the Thames, began to encroach beyond the waterline and one of its effects was to accentuate the penetrating echo from our horse's hoofs. Mercifully, Wiggins grabbed Holmes's coat sleeve at this moment and Holmes tapped softly on the roof of the cab. King promptly brought us to a halt.

Holmes ushered Wiggins from the cab and as he closed the door behind them he asked the rest of us to await his return.

'I shall return for you once I have established that the way ahead is clear. King, it is imperative that you keep your noble beast as still and as silent as he is at the moment.' Holmes ran his hand along the horse's long and matted mane and, with the gangly urchin leading the way, the two of them were soon swallowed up by the all-embracing fog, which was thickening by the minute.

King had ensured that we were some way from a gas lamp when he had eventually pulled over, so that my watch was rendered useless in the near-darkness. I could, therefore, only guess as to the length of time that Holmes was away from the cab, but it certainly appeared to be considerably longer than the thirty minutes that he had subsequently assured me that it had been.

The tense and stilted silence within the cab was eventually broken by the sound of soft, muffled footsteps, which were coming towards us from the direction of the river. We assumed that the sound came from the feet of Holmes and Wiggins; however, we were still much relieved at the sight of Holmes's smiling and eager face as he presented it through the open cab window.

'Stealth and absolute silence are of the absolute essence if we are to thwart our opponent with the minimum of effort,' Holmes warned us as he beckoned us from the cab with a crook of his finger.

It was decided that 'Gunner' King was to remain at the ready with his cab, so that we were prepared for the eventuality of needing an urgent departure. The former artillery man pulled up his muffler and tugged down his cap as he set himself for what might have proved to be a lengthy vigil. Before we set off Holmes dispatched young Wiggins to return home, or to whichever door way would serve as one that night. We stood watching him flit from corner to corner, skilfully avoiding the glare of the gas lights, until we were certain that he was safely away from the area. Then we turned our attention to the river front and the matter at hand.

Naturally Holmes led the way, followed by Lestrade, Collier, myself, with Sergeant Rutherford holding back by a few yards at the rear. As far as the rest of us were concerned Holmes was surely leading us into the dark unknown. Every one of the narrow and cobbled alleyways that we were creeping along seemed to become ever darker and narrower as they sloped away before us towards the docks.

The thickening fog rendered the cobble stones damp and treacherous and they seemed to become looser and further apart the more we progressed. Consequently it became increasingly difficult for us to maintain a sure footing and I, for one, lost mine on several occasions. The sound of barges setting off their warning horns gradually became more frequent and, though muffled by the fog, noticeably louder.

The need for a cautious silence was now more obvious than ever before and when Sergeant Rutherford could no longer contain his raw booming cough, Holmes turned and glared a warning in his direction. The big man mumbled an embarrassed apology and wrapped his scarf around his mouth.

In this manner we continued for a few more yards until Holmes indicated that he wanted us to crouch down low as a further precaution against being seen. We followed his lead and our progress became yet slower and more uncomfortable. At last Holmes raised his hand above his head, which indicated that he wanted our tiny column to come to a halt.

We immediately closed up behind him, apart from Rutherford who continued to hold back. Holmes pointed towards a ramshackle, disused warehouse, which was situated directly upon the water's edge. It was a red brick, two-storey building, whose metal roof was much corroded by mist and its large wooden door was only connected to its frame by a single hinge.

To the right of the building I could just make out the distinctive and ghostly outline of the *Matilda Briggs*. I watched for a moment while the chill breeze blowing up from the estuary was causing the fog to dance around the tips of the ship's bare masts in strange spectral patterns.

Berthed to the left of the steam clipper could be seen the smaller shape of a schooner. We subsequently discovered that she was the *Bellerophon*, the very ship upon which Tilat had arranged to escape. We could make out activity on the deck, which confirmed Wiggins's assertion that she was planning a dawn departure; we could only hope that Tilat had not yet taken up his berth. A moment later we realized that our fears were unfounded.

'It would seem that Wiggins has surely hit the mark,' Holmes whispered. 'See, even now a light burning inside the hut is clearly visible.'

Sure enough, we could just make out the dull orange glow of an oil flame seeping out around the edges of the precarious door. We all exchanged glances of relief, for we now realized that the object of our stealthy visit was undoubtedly still at home!

'Watson and I will now approach the warehouse door,' Holmes said, also indicating that my revolver should be at the ready by glancing towards the pocket of my overcoat.

'That task should surely fall to Rutherford and myself, seeing as we are the only members of the official force presently on the scene.' However, Lestrade's barely audible objections were irrelevant as Holmes was already halfway to the warehouse entrance and I was close on his heels. I fingered my revolver repeatedly as I crept up behind him and laid a firm grip upon its handle the moment Holmes had placed his hand upon the surface of the door.

From the very instant that the door began to move we realized that any hope that we might have had of catching the room's occupant unawares was surely lost. Despite Holmes's extreme caution there was no disguising the shuddering shriek that the rusty hinge immediately emitted. Holmes changed his tack at once and with a full swing of his boot he sent the door hurling to the ground with an almighty crash!

The remainder of our party caught up with us without delay and, with weapons drawn, we all entered the warehouse ready and prepared for the inevitable confrontation. I would not say that we were actually disappointed when this did not occur, because we each let out a deep sigh of released tension, once we had realized that the room was completely empty. Nevertheless it was disheartening to recognize that all of our efforts at apprehending Tilat appeared to have been thwarted at the very moment of our anticipated success.

It was left to Holmes to raise our flagging spirits once more.

'Do not distress yourselves unduly, gentlemen, for all is not yet lost,' he announced with an anticipatory smile.

'How can you make such a statement?' I turned on Holmes irritably. 'The man we are after is nowhere to be seen!'

'You know my method, Watson, and when I say to you that Tilat is still within our reach, you should know that I am not making an empty gesture of encouragement. Look around you and observe.'

Holmes raised the flap at the front of his lantern to add to the light generated by the small oil lamp in the far corner of the room.

The extra illumination revealed very little to me. The damp empty chamber was chill from neglect, and the plaster was crumbling away from its warped walls. A few broken tea chests were scattered around the room, their contents emptied or decomposed long ago. Then I noticed a small bundle, held together with string, that was lying on the floor close to the lamp. There was every indication that it might have been a collection of personal belongings. There was nothing more.

'I can see nothing that would raise my expectations.' I shook my head dejectedly.

'Look at the remains of the oil in the lamp, Watson. Can you not see that it is almost full?'

'Of course! The lamp has only been alight for a few minutes,' I declared.

'That and the fact that his meagre luggage is still here means that Tilat must be very close by. We would have noticed him if he had attempted to board the schooner,' Holmes added.'

'Perhaps we should examine his belongings while we have the opportunity?' Lestrade suggested.

As usual Holmes was a step ahead of the official detective and he had already positioned his lamp on the floor next to the bundle when Sergeant Rutherford suddenly burst in upon us.

'You had better come quickly and have a look at this,' he called. 'I do not know what to make of it, I am sure.'

Holmes jumped up from the floor and we all followed Rutherford back outside.

We found him pointing towards the rooftop of an adjacent warehouse that was no more than a stone's throw away from the *Bellerophon*. Every so often a glimpse of the three-quarter moon was revealed by a momentary clearing in the constantly shifting fog. We followed the line of Rutherford's arm and as the moon was revealed, for the briefest of instants, its cold, silvery light highlighted a startling sight.

There, turning this way and that and resembling for all the world a primeval animal hopelessly trapped within a jungle fire, was the diabolical sight of the man in the crimson robe!

I could not understand how a man as clever and resourceful as Tilat undoubtedly was, could have allowed himself to fall into so precarious a situation. I could only presume that he been attempting to reach the *Bellerophon* before her departure, but had then discovered that his route to the schooner had been cut off by one of the steam launches that Lestrade had put into position for that very purpose. We were subsequently informed that this had indeed been so.

The glare from the moon highlighted the remarkable figure of this robed rebel leader, perfectly. He stood out in relief against the background of the London skyline and I realized that he would be an easy target for my revolver at so short a distance. I slowly removed my weapon from its pocket and was on the point of training it upon Tilat, when a strong hand pushed downwards upon its barrel.

'No, Watson. We have much still to learn from this remarkable man and it would be wrong to deprive ourselves of the opportunity of doing so. Besides, we are not even certain, as yet, of the exact circumstances that led to the tragedy aboard the *Matilda Briggs*. Tilat may be guilty of nothing more than trying to protect himself. He may have killed only in self-defence. With the knowledge that we now have of Mandel's true character, it would not be entirely unlikely if that proves to be the case.'

'Mr Holmes, surely you are not suggesting that we are to allow a suspected multiple killer to escape?' Lestrade asked excitedly.

'No, Inspector, I am suggesting nothing of the sort. Remember that there are many different ways of skinning a cat.'

'Then what exactly are you proposing?'

I noticed, with some consternation that, before answering Lestrade's question, Holmes removed his coat and then his jacket and tie. He then strode purposefully towards a frail metal ladder that was attached to the building upon which Tilat had now trapped himself.

I ran towards him and attempted to hold him back.

'Holmes, I really must protest,' I called out. 'Surely this time you risk too much!'

Lestrade ran over and voiced his own concerns, but Holmes remained resolute and would not bow to our entreaties.

'Do not be too alarmed. After all, if my baritsu form of Japanese wrestling was able to account for Colonel Moriarty, I am certain that it will prove itself to be more than a match for this master of silat.' Holmes smiled reassuringly as he began to climb.

'I beseech you not to shoot unless we are faced with the most dire of circumstances.' Holmes's voice echoed down to me, but even as I put my gun away, I remained unconvinced by his declaration and my hand remained clenched upon my pistol inside my pocket.

We all moved back so that we could observe clearly the events upon the roof, although I made sure that I remained within a comfortable shooting distance. At one point it seemed as though Tilat was contemplating making a perilous leap from his roof to one that was a full twenty yards away! However, once he realized that Holmes was climbing towards him, he abandoned that extreme measure and moved across in order to confront Holmes at the head of the ladder. He realized that at that precise moment Holmes would be at his most vulnerable.

Fortunately Holmes was also aware of that possibility and he hesitated, once he had reached the head of the ladder, before lifting himself on to the roof itself. Holmes explained to me afterwards that silat was a martial art that was similar in many ways to the Chinese art of kung fu. Its origins could be traced back over a thousand years to the Indian Himalayas and it was as much a spiritual discipline as a physical one. This explained Tilat's next action.

Instead of attacking Holmes as soon as he had reached the top of the ladder, Tilat stood quite still and upright while he moved his arms forward and upwards in a series of slow controlled movements. This form of standing meditation was Tilat's way of drawing in and controlling his chi or, in other words, the universal force that is all around us. Finally he removed his straw sandals with great care.

This moment of hesitation, no matter how crucial it had been to Tilat's preparation, allowed Holmes the chance to gain the rooftop unhindered. He turned towards us, momentarily, and the thrill of an impending battle clearly flared like living flames in his eyes. He then turned to face his opponent.

By this time Tilat had concluded his meditation and he was now practising his own particular form of silat, which he had based upon the movements and the mannerisms of the Sumatran rat monkey. Of course, my only experience of monkeys had been limited to my observations within the zoological gardens of Regent's Park. However I could not fail to notice how uncannily akin to our simian cousins Tilat's movements undoubtedly were.

Unlike Holmes's baritsu wrestling, many of Tilat's movements were ground-based, and as he slowly made his way towards Holmes he would occasionally drop to the ground and swing his legs around in swift circular movements. Holmes stood defiantly before him and raised his palms ahead of him, in readiness for the initial attack.

At that moment Tilat let out a startling and deafening battle cry that chilled us all to the core as it echoed around the cold and deserted docks. Clearly this cry did not have the desired effect upon Holmes's determination, for he continued to face Tilat down. Yet, despite his intense concentration, Holmes was caught completely unawares by Tilat's first ploy.

Tilat threatened with the palms of his hands, in a manner

similar to that described by Michael Collier, when he mentioned the caged rat monkey in Tilat's Sumatran camp. Holmes countered that with a thrust of his own, but was unprepared for a sudden swing from Tilat's left leg.

Tilat caught Holmes on his right calf with a sickening crunch and although he did not fall Holmes was clearly caught off balance. This allowed Tilat the opportunity to move in with a strike of his palm to Holmes's shoulder. All that Holmes could do was fend it off with a wrist-hold of his own. Holmes's style relied almost entirely on close contact and holds, but Tilat's constant circular motions, which were fluid and almost balletic, made this virtually impossible.

Once or twice Holmes did manage to manoeuvre himself inside Tilat's guard and force a grip upon one of his arms, but on each occasion, with a simple floating turn, Tilat managed to extricate himself again and then launch a fresh attack of his own. Instinctively and not without a tinge of guilt, I felt my grip upon my revolver becoming ever tighter.

Holmes's normally well-groomed hair was constantly falling down over his eyes and as he pushed it back, time and again, I noticed that there was evidence of numerous facial cuts and bruises that were beginning to swell around his eyes. The constant barrage of swift and subtle blows that Tilat was raining down upon him was clearly beginning to take its toll upon my friend and he seemed to have no suitable response.

Gradually a pattern seemed to be emerging, in which Tilat was slowly manoeuvring Holmes towards the edge of the rooftop. At one point Holmes was actually teetering on the roof's very edge and he was balancing on the balls of his feet! I was on the point of releasing a volley from my revolver when Holmes miraculously launched himself into a overhead leap that saw him crash to the floor in a position of safety. With a feeling of intense relief I eased my finger away from the trigger. It seemed as if Holmes's final instructions were still controlling my actions, although I was obeying them with some reluctance.

Tilat would have been on to him in an instant; however Holmes managed to spring to his feet in time, then, in an act of extreme desperation, he hurled his entire body towards that of his opponents. A simple twist of his waist was all that Tilat needed to execute in order to avoid the impact of Holmes's frantic attack. Then, inexplicably, Tilat stopped in his tracks.

He stood upright once more and went through the same ritual that he had displayed at the beginning of the battle. His bearing and posture were imperious as he stood there composing himself for what would be his final onslaught. Holmes stood before him, defiant and fearless to the last and yet clearly overwhelmed by the extraordinary skills and powers of an undoubted master of his art. As a sign of his respect for Holmes's bravery, Tilat slowly bowed his head towards him.

Then Tilat let up another of his chilling battle cries and began to execute another series of his deadly circular movements and palm thrusts. Each one of these seemed to find their mark and by now Holmes was capable of offering little or no resistance!

Their progress towards the roof's edge was swifter and unhindered this time. Holmes looked over his shoulder repeatedly as he sensed the chill oblivion that surely now awaited him. His battered body swayed this way and that and Tilat's attack was remorseless. I remembered Holmes's words and decided that these were 'dire circumstances' indeed.

Then, and to my intense surprise, when I was at the very point of releasing my bullets, Holmes's strident voice echoed out once more.

'In heaven's name, do not shoot!'

Even now, when the preservation of my friend's life was my sole object and all other hope was lost, the effect that his voice had upon my actions was absolute. I lowered my revolver once more, at the very instant that a younger and steadier hand than mine had fired off a volley of his own. The bullet from Daniel Collier's revolver had caught Tilat cleanly in the centre of his throat.

With a blood-curdling cry the man in the crimson robe clutched both hands to his fatal wound. He was forced to spin around, by the momentum of the shot and, without another sound, he disappeared over the edge of the roof and into the dark abyss!

CHAPTER TWELVE

THE FINAL LETTER

The manner in which Collier had allowed his weapon to drop from his hand and then the anger with which he had kicked it away from himself, once it had landed on the slippery stones at his feet, seemed to suggest to me that this had been the first occasion on which he had been required to use his revolver in anger. The idea of taking another life was clearly abhorrent to him; he turned pale and quickly ran to a nearby drain down which he vomited uncontrollably.

However, my immediate concern was not with the well-being of the young archaeologist, who had still many lessons to learn, about both life and death. For my bruised and battered friend was lying prostrate on a rooftop above me; he was clearly in need of my attention. I lost no time in ascending the ladder and I was by his side in an instant.

To my relief and great surprise I discovered that Holmes was still conscious by the time that I had reached him. He smiled weakly as soon as he recognized me. It did not take me long to ascertain that many of his injuries were most severe and I could only offer a prayer of thanks that Holmes had not met the same fate as that of Carl Mandel.

I cursed myself for having embarked on such a mission without having brought my bag with me. I immediately called down to Rutherford and asked him to dispatch 'Gunner' King to

Baker Street, so that he might collect it for me without a moment's delay.

'In heaven's name, Holmes, why did you allow yourself to come to this? To forbid me to shoot was sheer folly,' I protested once I had returned to his side. He grimaced most grotesquely when I informed him that it had been Collier who had fired the fatal shot at Tilat. It was all I could do to prevent him from trying to raise himself from the floor.

His voice was hoarse and weak; therefore, he grabbed at my collar and pulled me close to his mouth so that I could hear him.

'Do you not see? I had at last managed to penetrate the veil!' Even in this semi-conscious state Holmes could not avoid being anything less than enigmatic. His meaning was not clear to me. Perhaps he was suffering from a mild touch of delirium? Nevertheless, the effort that he had expended in making this point to me was evidently more than his ravaged constitution could bear and he fainted quietly away.

I folded my overcoat and placed it gently beneath his head. Once I was satisfied that he was as comfortable as he could be, I stood up and lit a cigarette.

This strange and fateful dawn had, by now, daubed everything around me with a sepia hue. The fog was still dense, yet the *Matilda Briggs* had assumed a most surreal aspect that only added to its mystery. The barges in the distance seemed to float in and out of the folds of rolling mists and their horns were the only sound that pierced the gloom.

Then the call of excited voices rose up from the decks of the *Bellerophon* as the crew came up to discover the cause of all of the commotion. They could not know that their mysterious passenger's demise was the cause of this ensuing mayhem. Then a familiar voice rang out above all of the others.

Inspector Lestrade had assumed control over the police launches and he was now directing the operation to recover Tilat's body. He was clearly in his element and could already, no doubt, see the headlines in the next day's papers! I smiled to myself as the pitch of his voice rose in proportion to his increasing agitation.

By now Collier had recovered sufficiently for him to be able to join me on the roof top together with Sergeant Rutherford. It was not without some difficulty that we three managed to manoeuvre Holmes back down to street level without causing him further harm. Holmes remained unconscious throughout and by the time we had reached Tilat's hideaway King had returned with my medical bag.

We had found some sacking in a corner of the warehouse and proceeded to lay Holmes carefully upon it. I set to work immediately with some iodine and swabs and soon realized that Holmes's wounds were not as severe as I had at first feared them to be. The sharp effect of the iodine upon his open wounds soon brought Holmes back to full consciousness and, with surprising co-operation on his part, I managed to find the areas that were causing him the most discomfort and pain. Of course, the healing of his ribs would have to take its full and natural course.

The pain from his ribs, on each occasion that he coughed, soon put paid to any inclination that Holmes might have had to smoke. However I had fortunately brought along a flask full of brandy and I fed this to Holmes in copious amounts. The alcohol soon had the desired effect and in a short while Holmes felt able to turn his attention towards the bundle that comprised Tilat's abandoned luggage.

Tilat surely lived most frugally, for his baggage contained nothing of note. A simple change of clothes and a spare pair of straw sandals made up his wardrobe and these had been arranged so as to protect two small oilskin packets. As he delicately fingered each object Holmes gave the impression that he already had a good idea of what he was likely to find inside them.

At that point a rather excited Inspector Lestrade strode triumphantly into the room.

'We have him!' he declared. 'We shall have to lay him down in here for a while, I am afraid, until the wagon has arrived for him. He is an absolute giant of a man, you know, and it is taking three of my best men to struggle over here with him!'

Then he noticed Holmes, who was bending over in the corner.

'How is our friend progressing, Doctor?' Lestrade whispered anxiously.

'I thank you for your concern, Inspector, but I can assure you that I am more than capable of answering on my own behalf! I have suffered a few minor cuts and bruises and nothing more.'

'A few cuts and bruises indeed! You took an almighty beating, Holmes, and young Collier's timely intervention prevented it from becoming something far worse than that. You really must take care, you know.' I said this while knowing full well the futility of making such a suggestion.

'Yes indeed, we really must congratulate you, young man.' Lestrade addressed Collier. 'You displayed a cool head and a steady arm, as I am certain that Mr Holmes will readily and grate-fully acknowledge.'

Holmes smiled briefly and mumbled something incoherently under his breath. With some effort and a display of discomfort, Holmes slowly stood up again. He was now holding the two oilskin packets, but he appeared to be strangely reluctant to open either of them. To my dismay Holmes lit himself a cigarette, then struggled to suppress the inevitable and painful cough that it induced.

'Your wounds will never heal themselves if you treat them in such a cavalier fashion,' I protested.

Holmes placed his right forefinger over his pursed lips and moved towards the doorway to await the arrival of Tilat's body, while still clinging on to the two curious packets.

The three burly constables were indeed struggling beneath the weight of the sodden corpse, and I wasted no time in offering my assistance as they laid him down upon the bed of sacking that

Holmes had so recently vacated. We were all taken aback by Tilat's dramatic appearance; even in death he seemed to command respect and reverence.

His striking robe was soaked through and reeked with the stench that it had collected from the river Thames. His head covering did chillingly invoke the vision of death that Carl Mandel had alluded to before he died. It was still clearly etched with a representation of the Sumatran rat monkey that Tilat had so vividly emulated with his silat movements.

Holmes appeared to be strangely pensive and hesitant before, at last, he requested that I remove Tilat's unusual head-wear. Sergeant Rutherford led his constables outside and we four fell into a deferential silence as I moved the oil lamp across the room to the side of the corpse. The muted orange light cast a gigantic shadow of the dead rebel leader upon the adjacent wall, and the removal of his mask felt strangely intrusive to me.

I was able to peel it away without any great difficulty; however, the face that was revealed was far removed from the one that I had pictured in my mind's eye. I glanced around at my companions to see if this revelation was having the same effect upon them. Evidently Lestrade had built up no such picture, for he appeared to be unmoved and indifferent.

Holmes's face clouded over and he suddenly turned his head away from the sight, as if greatly pained by a stark realization, although not entirely surprised by it.

Daniel Collier's reaction was as dramatic as it had been unexpected. The colour in his face became as ashen as that of the dead man himself and, with a haunting moan of lament, he fainted clean away and he dropped on to the harsh ungiving floor!

My dear son Daniel, if you are reading this now and my final letter has not fallen into the hands of strangers, for whose eyes it was never intended, it surely signifies that I have failed in my attempts to reach you and entrust the beladau into your noble charge.

It would be unfair of me to bid you my final farewell without having first acquainted you with the events that have brought me to this sorry pass.

As I sat there, on the waters of Lake Toba, agonizing over my next course of action, it suddenly occurred to me that fate was leading me inexorably towards the rapids of the Alas river and the port town of Meulaboh. Having reached this conclusion I set off without a moment's further hesitation.

My journey home began under the most tranquil of circumstances. The waterfall, which emptied out of the lake at its most north-westerly outlet, was far less precipitous than the inlet that I had negotiated at Sipiso-Piso, and I therefore encountered no real difficulty in achieving my descent. Furthermore, the Alas showed no signs of living up to its fearsome reputation and I began to row effortlessly along its serene waters.

However, once I had negotiated a series of narrow and tree-lined gorges the Alas began to tilt dramatically towards the downlands. Rocky outcrops began to appear in the centre of the stream and I had to use my new oars, which the Ghadar had had constructed especially for this purpose, to fend myself away from them. As the pace of the river gradually increased this became more and more difficult.

My reinforced boat began to take a severe buffeting and during the course of a series of collisions one of my oars splintered into matchwood! I was now fighting a constant battle for survival and this intensified as the river transformed into a series of turbulent rapids. It needed constant effort to keep my boat afloat and on an even keel, and I prayed for at least a moment or two of relief. This was not to be granted.

As I drew closer to sea level the drops between each short level stretch of water became ever steeper and my remaining oar was rapidly becoming useless. Once again I found that my fate was to be consigned to the lap of the gods and I strapped myself to the bottom of my boat, there to await whatever outcome they had arranged for me.

It turned out that once again I had been blessed. My boat came to an abrupt halt as it collided into and became embedded in a soft sand bank, no more than a hundred yards away from the tiny port of Meulaboh. The size of the port belied the importance of the town itself. Meulaboh boasted a thriving fishing industry and the town itself comprised a colourful agglomeration of single-storey wooden buildings and its economic expansion was only limited by the shallowness of its harbour.

As you have already probably surmised, I managed to find a mail packet-ship that was homeward bound, and from the proceeds of the sale of my favourite compass I managed to secure a passage for myself aboard her all the way to war-torn Banda Aceh. Before embarking I decided to destroy and sink my tiny boat, in the hope that its remains might throw the Dutch off my trail, should they be pursuing me.

It might sound strange for you to hear, but as I holed her tiny hull I was riddled with regret and pangs of great sadness. After all, for so long now she had been my rudimentary home and at times my salvation.

Once the mail ship was well under way I decided to explain my dilemma to the ship's captain, a gruff red-faced Scotsman who sported a luxuriant white beard and went by the name of 'Father' Campbell. In truth, however, he could not have been further removed from a true man of the cloth. He seemed to curse with every other word that he hollered and drank thirstily from a bottle of Scotch whisky at every opportunity!

Of course I did not divulge to him the true nature of my mission, although the explanation of my plight was sufficient to gain his sympathy and co-operation. He was equally generous with his bottle and over a glass of two, on our first night out, he told me of a deep inlet within a half-mile of Aceh harbour, where he could set me down and thereby avoid any unwanted attention when we arrived at the main harbour.

This proposal suited me very well and allowed me the chance to enter Aceh under cover of darkness. I entrusted my third letter to you into the hands of Captain Campbell and, confident that his final port of call was to be the port of London, I disembarked at the prearranged location.

There had been rumours of how the fighting between the Dutch and the Sultanate's guerrilla forces had been dying down in recent days and as I approached the thinly populated outer suburbs of Aceh I was relieved to find that I had had no reason to doubt them. In the distance, towards the more built-up areas close to the harbour, I did notice the dull red glow of smouldering buildings. These were few and far between, however and the sounds of gunfire were sporadic.

I felt my way along the silent and darkened streets in the hope that I might come across a place of shelter for the night. I was most fortunate in that I managed to gain the trust of a street wise young urchin who went by the name of Shamir. Without a moment's hesitation he led me to a burnt-out building which he had ingeniously converted into a rudimentary home for himself from the surrounding rubble.

I had to sacrifice my last remaining item of any value, the gold pendant that had been presented to me by the Royal Society upon my return from East Africa. However such an object would probably enable Shamir to survive a full year upon the streets of his war-scarred home and for this he was willing and able to assist me in any way that I needed.

The following morning, shortly after he had brought me a nourishing breakfast of fruits, Shamir set off at once for the port to see if there was any news of London-bound shipping. When he returned that evening he shook his head sadly because he sincerely felt that he had let me down. Unfortunately this became a pattern, repeated throughout the ensuing days and I was beginning to believe that my letter would arrive so far in advance of me that you would begin to harbour grave doubts for my welfare.

Then one day Shamir arrived with the most tragic news imaginable, although, of course, he had no way of knowing its true significance to me. The Dutch were celebrating the defeat of the brave and noble Tilat and his men at the Battle of the Lake. Tilat's body was being shipped back to India as a gesture of goodwill towards the British. I did not wish the boy to witness the effect that this news was having upon me and so I decided to take myself for a walk. A walk that lasted until well after dawn!

By the time I had returned to Shamir's shelter I was filled with the same resolve to return Tilat's beladau safely to London, even though my motives for so doing were now vastly different. One day, perhaps, a new leader would emerge who would have need of this symbol of his people's freedom. In the meantime I would entrust it into your care, my dear boy, for there is no one else in whom I would bestow this sacred trust without a moment's doubt.

The following evening Shamir returned home with better news.

A cousin of his, named Shivam, who was employed at the docks, had heard of an American-registered steam clipper that had made an unscheduled stop on its way from Calcutta to London. She was carrying her usual cargo of tea, but this commodity was in relatively short supply, as a result of a prolonged drought and she wished to fill her hold with as much black pepper as she could secure.

This she was well able to do in a marketplace such as Aceh, which always seemed to have a surplus. Shivam had also heard of a rumour that concerned a cache of illicit Dutch gold and a young American merchant who had associates within the Meuligo, or the Dutch governor's pavilion. Although these stories had so far remained unsubstantiated, every one of Shivam's fellow workers at the docks were surprised at the clipper's proposed early departure and the furtive behaviour of the crew.

For now, however, they were preparing themselves for the long voyage home by visiting everyone of the notorious watering holes with which Banda Aceh so plentifully abounds. Shivam quite correctly reasoned that this would present me with the perfect opportunity for stowing myself away in the hold of the *Matilda Briggs*.

The two cousins supplied me with enough provisions for my expected prolonged seclusion before leading me through a labyrinth of backstreets and alleyways that were seldom used, on our way down to the harbour. Sadly we passed by the burnt-out husk of what had once been the magnificent Baiturrachman Mosque, before the Dutch had destroyed it during a reprisal against the Sultanate of Aceh in the 1880s.

By the time we had reached the docks it was in the dead of night and the crew of the *Matilda Briggs* had displayed no signs of having returned from their night of revelry. I was on the point of approaching the ship when we noticed that the ship's captain had at least displayed enough good sense to have installed a solitary guard to watch over their cargo, illicit or otherwise.

Shamir and his cousin volunteered to act as decoys while I climbed the short anchor rope and hopped silently on to the deck above. The boys wandered up the gangplank and diverted the guard by begging for food. They let up a most awful wailing noise until they were certain that I had secreted myself in the hold of the *Matilda Briggs*.

Until such time as I was certain that we were safely under way at sea, I decided to bury myself beneath the huge mountain of black pepper by which I was surrounded. Thereafter I would remain below decks for the duration of the voyage and stretch out my meagre provisions until the journey's end.

It will prove impossible for me to continue with my letter from now onwards, as the hold is almost entirely airtight, once the hatch is secured and therefore I will be confined in total darkness. However, my plans now appear to be coming to fruition and any further news that I might have for you can surely now be delivered in person!

I look forward to the moment when we can be together once again.

The empty warehouse was beginning to take on an atmosphere similar to that of my field tent during the Afghan campaign. Fortunately the wagon arrived shortly afterwards to remove the body. I deliberately withheld my smelling salts from Daniel Collier in order to spare him the trauma of seeing the body moved. In the meantime Holmes had began to remove the oilskin from the two packets.

The first and larger of the two contained one of the most beautifully crafted weapons that I have ever seen. It was every bit as remarkable as Sir Michael Collier had described it to be in his letter. As I lifted it by its red leather handle I was astounded by its weight and balance. Holmes confirmed that the inscriptions on the blade were in the form of a dedication to the Hindu god, Vishnu, and in the vernacular of ancient Sanskrit.

The object that I now held in awe was undoubtedly the famed beladau, which had proved to be Collier's holy grail and our worst fears were surely confirmed. Daniel Collier's reaction to the unmasking of the 'Giant Rat of Sumatra' was now of little surprise to us, for he had just inadvertently taken the life of his own long lost father!

Holmes was seated on the floor, close to where Collier was lying, shaking his head disconsolately while he held the other packet tightly in his grasp.

'We must not open this until we are safely back at Baker Street and our young friend here is better prepared to receive his late father's final words to him. Oh Watson! To think that I allowed this tragedy to come about.'

'You must not unjustly chastise yourself, Holmes. The events that led to this sorry culmination, occurred many thousands of miles away, and it is remarkable that you have discovered as much as you eventually did. We had no reason to suppose that it was anyone other than Tilat hidden behind that ghastly mask,' I ventured, fully aware of the fact that Sherlock Holmes was not normally a man who could be so easily consoled.

'There is no man alive who could have accomplished more,' Lestrade offered sincerely and from this source Holmes seemed to derive a little more comfort.

He secreted the packet in an inside pocket and lit up a cigarette while he brushed himself free from the dirt and dust that had adhered to him during his time spent on the floor. I administered some salts to Daniel Collier and, as he slowly returned to consciousness, I could swear that the absence of the corpse now convinced him that the sight of his father's dead body had been nothing more than a horrific apparition.

'I would gladly sacrifice myself a thousand times over if I thought that it would restore your father to you.' Holmes evidently felt that it would be best to dispel Collier's delusion at the earliest moment.

'So it is true,' Collier whispered as he slowly raised himself up from the floor.

'I truly wish that it were not so,' I said as I gently fed to him the last of the contents of my flask.

Collier was still undeniably shaken, and it took the three of us to help him climb aboard 'Gunner' King's cab, which was still waiting patiently for us on the corner.

'Inspector, I shall assume that you intend to join us at Baker Street,' Holmes observed sternly before he climbed aboard.

'Naturally, Mr Holmes. As you are all undoubtedly aware, although we are all witnesses to the circumstances of Sir Michael Collier's death, his son will still have to undergo the full and due legal processes before he is technically a free man. Although, of course, the conclusion is foregone. Besides, my report already promises to be so colourful and outrageous that any further information that I might learn from these letters will stand me in good stead.'

Acting upon Holmes's instructions, King ensured that the return journey was a far more sedate affair than the outward one had been. Indeed, by the time that we had eventually pulled up outside 221B Mrs Hudson was already awake and busy in her parlour.

Impatiently waving aside her offers of breakfast, Holmes slowly limped ahead of us up to our rooms, obviously still in some pain. He immediately reached for his pipe and tobacco and tore at the oilskin wrapping of the second package, to reveal not one but two hurriedly scrawled letters, signed in the dead explorer's distinctive hand.

Before requesting that I read from the longer of the two, Holmes sympathetically ensured that Daniel Collier was steady enough to hear his late father's final words. Collier took several deep breaths as he steeled himself for such an emotional ordeal and then nodded towards me slowly and emphatically.

I read quietly and deliberately; however by the time I had reached the last optimistic sentence young Collier had broken down again altogether. He appeared to be inconsolable and I led him through to Holmes's room before calling down to Mrs Hudson for some coffee for all of us.

'Do you know, Watson, that sometimes it seems to me that, no matter how good our intentions might truly be, our interference can lead to doing more harm than it does good. If we had allowed Collier to reach his son, by now he would have passed over the symbolic beladau and, in all probability, made good his escape, with nobody else any the worse off!' Holmes complained bitterly.

'Although you would have sacrificed your most precious of principles and relinquished your relentless pursuit of justice had you done so,' I reminded him.

At that moment Mrs Hudson arrived with our coffee. Collier walked slowly from Holmes's room, a moment or two later, still rubbing his reddened eyes and hunched at the shoulders. I offered him a cigarette to go with his coffee as he took his seat.

'I am ready now, gentlemen,' he stated simply, and Holmes gestured to me that I might now read from the second crumpled piece of parchment.

My dear son, I received news of your intention to seek a consultation with the remarkable Mr Sherlock Holmes by way of a wire sent to me by your landlady in St Ives. Therefore, I am certain that, by now, he has fully acquainted you with the events that led to the tragedy aboard the *Matilda Briggs*.

I beseech you not to judge me too harshly. Obviously I knew that I was doing wrong by stowing away illegally in the first place. However, I was in no doubt that I would have no great difficulty in making good my escape once the business of unloading the tea had begun. I little realized that the rumours regarding the illicit gold were well-founded and that the crew of the *Matilda Briggs* had no intention of even touching the tea. Nor the pepper for that matter.

Their intended docking position was ignored and it was only when I began to make out some of the instructions that were being shouted by the captain on deck that I realized the serious peril that my discovery would place me in. After all, there is a world of difference between the reaction of a tea importer from that of a gold smuggler, in such a situation.

I wasted little time in secreting myself once they had docked and, to save you the embarrassment of my dilemma becoming public knowledge, I decided to disguise myself in the robe and mask of the 'Giant Rat' in which Tilat had originally wrapped the beladau.

I strapped the beladau, wrapped in oilskin, to my belt and had every intention of going over the side in order to escape unnoticed. However, events moved far more quickly than I had envisaged that they would do and I was only half of the way up the stairs from the hold, when the hatch was flung open and I was confronted by the crew!

There was no escaping them from my precarious position on the stairs and so I allowed myself to be lifted up on to the deck by my arms. My wrists were then trussed up behind my back, with a piece of ship's cord and Captain Handley, as the crew addressed him, considered the best way of dealing with me. Evidently the offloading and delivery of the gold was a matter of far greater urgency, and I was left tied to a mast while they went about their nefarious deeds.

Since we were docked at St Katherine's, I can only assume that the gold was supposed to be delivered to a destination somewhere in the City. The scheme had been well thought out, because a small cart was already awaiting them. Once the cart had been fully loaded Handley returned with instructions that two members of the crew would remain with me on board and that they would join the others at the designated meeting point, when they had dealt with me.

Once the cart had departed I looked up and observed my two guards. One was a middle-aged able seaman, who wore the scars of his many years before the mast with a weary indifference. He clearly did not have the stomach for the task that had been set for him and had to be cajoled by his companion before he dragged me back up to my feet. This companion of his, whom I had heard referred to as Mandel, clearly relished the prospect of disposing of me. His round-faced and youthful countenance belied his inherent maliciousness and he withdrew his long blade with a malevolent glint in his eyes.

As he approached me with his gaze firmly fixed upon my throat, I employed one of the many leg strikes that I had recently been taught. I sent my right foot crunching into the able seaman's shin just below the knee. I did not need to be informed by that howl of his of the damage that I had done, because I could feel his bone crack clean through at the moment of impact. He fell writhing to the deck and rolled back and forth while he clutched his shattered limb. I had not realized, until it was almost too late, that while he had been holding his wound the able seaman was also sliding out a long thin knife that he had kept hidden down the side of his boot! Once again my resource was my foot and I brought this crashing down upon the side of the man's neck. The blow killed him at once.

Clearly feeling aghast at my appearance and the fearful injury that I had just wrought, Mandel became more hesitant and he held back for a moment or two. I dropped to the floor and swung my leg around, in the monkey style, so that it swept Mandel from his feet. He fell to the deck and although he was only momentarily stunned, this allowed me the time to take hold of his knife, which had spilled from his grasp, and I worked on my ropes with its glinting sharp blade.

I had not the time to sever the rope clean through, yet it had weakened sufficiently for me to able to tear it apart with a powerful jerk of my shoulders. With my hands now clear I felt prepared for Mandel's next move. Seemingly undaunted by my new-found freedom and the damage that I had exacted upon his friend, Mandel came towards me once more and I noticed that he was slowly pulling a small revolver from his inside pocket!

Before he had the opportunity to cock it, my left hand crashed against his wrist. As the weapon fell harmlessly away from him I lunged forward and my iron palm struck him cleanly upon a pressure point in his neck.

I had not intended to kill him, nor was I even certain at that moment that I had done so. However I could see that he was fighting for his life and would not be capable of any form of movement for some time to come. At that moment I became aware that the ship was slowly drifting away from its original moorings! Evidently Captain Handley, in his efforts to dissociate the *Matilda Briggs* from St Katherine's, had untied her before he had departed in the cart in the belief that the high morning tides would carry her away downstream.

I hurriedly carved a clue as to what had occurred into the decking with Mandel's blade. I inscribed it in Sanskrit in order to bolster the belief that Tilat had been behind the killings. I hauled the seaman's body over the side, and the revolver, together with Mandel's knife followed it into the chill, murky waters shortly afterwards.

I was on the point of checking Mandel for a pulse when I realized that the gap between the ship and the wharf was rapidly expanding. Soon it would be too late for me to make my escape. I leapt up on to the handrail and made the jump to the shore with barely half an inch to spare! I teetered on the edge of the embankment with my clenched toes and threw myself forward on to my face, to avoid an icy drenching.

My predicament was clear and I lost little time in sprinting away from the scene of my crime as the *Matilda Briggs* began to disappear round the bend of the river, becoming clouded by the early-morning mists. As you are now doubtless aware, I was fortunate in coming upon a deserted warehouse in a spot that was ideal for my purpose. I soon discovered that a small schooner, the *Bellerophon* was taking on crew and would be departing for the Far East within the next few days.

In the time remaining to me I have decided to channel my every effort into seeing you, my dear boy, for one last time. This, however, has proved to be no easy task. Your Mr Sherlock Holmes seems to have erected a cordon around us both that has proved to be impenetrable. Indeed, during my last attempt at gaining access to you, I was almost apprehended by an associate of his, a man who appears to be shadowing my every move. Mr Holmes's minions seem to be everywhere. There is no escaping them and they are closing in upon my hideaway even as I sit here in my warehouse writing this to you.

Once I am safely out of harm's way I will instruct my solicitors to dispose of my property in a manner that is beneficial to both you and our beloved Charlotte. In the meantime I can only leave you my letters and the sacred trust of Tilat's beladau, both of which you will find here at the appropriate time. I sincerely hope and pray that my timely departure will spare you the ignominy of having your father's infamous deeds being made public knowledge. The imminent departure of the *Bellerophon* certainly makes this seem most likely.

Have faith that my true intentions were always for the common good, however they might subsequently be misconstrued. Nonetheless, I have committed a grievous sin in the eyes of God and I am imprisoned within a nightmare of my own creation. So now I intend to journey once more to the hills of northern India, there to throw myself upon the mercy of the great masters and the grace of the most supreme soul.

You have always made me proud, my dear boy, and I regret
that my actions will have made it impossible for you to recipro-
cate those feelings. God speed.

As ever yours,

MC

It seemed strange that such an emotive letter should conclude in
so formal a style. However, Daniel Collier seemed oblivious to this
anomaly and he was greatly moved by his father's final words.
Neither Holmes nor I could think of a suitable response, and
Collier slowly rose and stared out from our window with such
intensity that he seemed to be searching for his father's image in
the swirling, angry clouds outside.

Lestrade mumbled apologetically about having to conclude the
necessary formalities, but added graciously that he would leave
that for a later time, to spare the young man any further grief.
Then he silently took his leave.

'I shall forever blame myself for my father's death,' Collier said
disconsolately and without turning towards us.

'You really should not,' Holmes stated simply. 'It is hard enough
for you to face such a tragic loss without further burdening yourself with feelings of guilt. If anybody should be blamed it is myself
and my own ineptitude.'

The next hour or so passed in a melancholy silence. At last
Collier stood up to take his leave. He shook Holmes and me
warmly by the hand before doing so.

'I can assure you, Mr Holmes, that I attach no blame to you for
the outcome of this affair. I shall forever remember you for your
kindness and your bravery. Before I leave I should like to entrust
the beladau into the care of the only men I know with whom its
secret will remain secure.'

Holmes bowed in acknowledgement of the honour and deliberately placed the beladau in the top drawer of his desk, to rest

alongside a few of his more treasured memorabilia. He attached the key to his watch chain.

'What do you intend to do next?' I asked the young man before he had the chance to reach the door.

He thought long and hard before making his reply.

'Once I have satisfied Inspector Lestrade's superiors at Scotland Yard, I shall ensure that my father is buried with full honour and respect. Then I shall seek out the only family member who is still left to me, my sweet sister, Charlotte. I shall endeavour to make my peace with her and then devote the rest of my life to doing good with the proceeds of my father's estate. In that sense our family will be together once again.'

'I can assure you that you will experience no difficulty in concluding the police formalities satisfactorily. Please kindly inform us once the arrangements for your father have been made,' Holmes asked earnestly.

Collier nodded emphatically before donning his absurd green headgear once again. He walked from the room a broken but determined young man, and I felt certain that he would, somehow, find his sister in the depths of Africa.

'What a remarkable young man and what a heavy and awful burden he now has to carry,' I said quietly once we had heard the street door close behind him.

'Indeed, heavier even than my own.' Holmes clearly had no intention of taking any of our words of resolution to heart and instead barricaded himself inside his room, together with a full ounce of tobacco, for the next forty-eight hours. Neither the entreaties of Mrs Hudson or myself could persuade Holmes to bring his self-imposed vigil to an early conclusion. It was only news of the Collier funeral that eventually roused him, and when he did at last emerge from his room he appeared to be both haggard and emaciated.

For once I refrained from my customary chastisement of his

flagrant self-abuse and offered him my full support at Collier's graveside. We bade Collier our final farewells and, on our return to Baker Street, Holmes resumed his doleful meditation in the confines of his room.

It was only when a letter eventually arrived, bearing a Cape Town postmark, that Holmes at last displayed any interest in events other than those inside his head. He smiled gratefully at my continued tolerance and insisted that I read the letter to him without delay. He assured me that he would eat properly once he had heard it all the way through. Obviously, I agreed to his terms at once.

My dear friends, Mr Sherlock Holmes and Doctor Watson,

Once again I must thank you both for your strength and support at my father's lamentably ill attended funeral. It would seem that, despite all of our efforts, his small-minded friends and colleagues could not accept our explanations once the newspapers had made the story of the 'Matilda Briggs' tragedy, public knowledge. Heaven only knows how they got hold of the story, but it would seem that the sense of justice that the authorities hold so dear does not extend to human dignity. Thankfully I will never have to encounter such bigotry again.

My journey to Natal was fortunately far smoother and less arduous than the one that my poor father had to endure. I followed the trail that my father outlined in his letter and discovered that Lieutenant Marcus Harrison was every bit as helpful and co-operative as my father had described him to be.

With his directions and the use of his cart, I found my way to the mission of Lovedale with no great difficulty. There the Reverend Joseph Stewart gave me precise instructions as to how I should be able to find my sister's mission in Matabeleland. I cannot express in mere words the sheer joy that Charlotte and I shared at our first meeting.

She was able to accept the circumstances of our father's death without a moment's hesitation or recrimination, for which I was most grateful, and she welcomed my arrival here with a warm and open heart.

It did not take me long to understand the reasons for Charlotte's desire to work here and only a little longer for me to see why she wished to remain. In the five years since the conclusion of the wars of annexation the Ndebele people have embraced a more peaceful way of life. Their pure and simple faith is awe-inspiring and has proved to be a constant source of inspiration for Charlotte and me. I have discovered a far greater fulfilment from working alongside these people, than ever I received from tinkering around with neolithic stones!

Admittedly the structure of the place is sadly rudimentary, especially the dejected-looking church. However, we are convinced that once the proceeds of our father's estate eventually arrive, we shall be able to bring about a complete transformation. I believe that it will be many years before my beloved England will see me again.

I am convinced that the manner in which Charlotte and I are able to work together is something that our parents would have wholeheartedly approved of and I hope that you can see how the horrors of that night at Canary Wharf have resulted in something good. This thought has proved to be my very salvation and I sincerely hope, Mr Holmes, that it will, eventually, become your consolation.

My best wishes to you both,
Daniel Collier.

I placed the letter carefully back upon the table and we sat in a reflective silence for a moment or two, after we had lit our pipes. I could tell from my friend's expression that the final sentiments of the letter were having an immediate effect upon him and when he did at last speak his voice had regained some of its former authority.

'It would seem that the death of their father has, at last, brought the Collier family together once more. It is also gratifying to know that, from the most extraordinary of circumstances, young Collier has found the peace of mind that others spend their entire lives trying to achieve,' he stated simply.

'From so much evil some good does indeed seem to have emerged,' I agreed.

'Ah, but where, in reality, was the evil? Certainly in the killer and blackmailer Carl Mandel. However, Declan McCrory was nothing more than a miscreant trying to save his business and protect the honour of his family. Whilst Sir Michael Collier and Tilat were both actors upon a far larger stage, who had become victims of their own circumstances. From what we have seen and experienced I do not think that either of them can be accurately described as evil.'

'Perhaps not, although that could very much depend upon one's political point of view,' I ventured.

'So, Watson, you are still not convinced of Collier's integrity?'

'Not so much that, but I do feel that he allowed certain events to cloud his better judgement. However, I would agree that he was certainly not an evil man.'

At that point Mrs Hudson arrived with our long awaited breakfast of curried eggs and, true to his word, Holmes moved across to the table, where he made short work of his first real food for days. Once the breakfast things had been cleared away we moved over to the fire and Holmes began to tune his violin. I picked up my notebook and pencil and turned the first page. Holmes placed a restraining hand upon my right arm.

'No, Watson, you should allow those ghosts to rest for a while before you resurrect them. I do not think that your public is yet ready for such a tale,' Holmes quietly suggested.

I took heed of his recommendation and picked up a daily paper instead. Once he was satisfied with his tuning Holmes returned to the Bruch concerto that he had started to play, it seemed, an eternity ago. The notes that floated from his instrument were so sublime and lyrical that I was at once convinced that his full presence of mind had returned to him.

This boded well indeed and I was now confident that Holmes would be prepared for any future challenges that might present themselves.

NOTES: